N'ice Shows

A Berrien Gamble Ice Skating Mystery

Joan Bartlett

Writers Club Press
San Jose New York Lincoln Shanghai

N'ice Shows
A Berrien Gamble Ice Skating Mystery

All Rights Reserved © 2000 by Joan Bartlett

No part of this book may be reproduced or transmitted in any form or by any means, graphic, electronic, or mechanical, including photocopying, recording, taping, or by any information storage or retrieval system, without the permission in writing from the publisher.

Published by Writers Club Press
an imprint of iUniverse.com, Inc.

For information address:
iUniverse.com, Inc.
620 North 48th Street
Suite 201
Lincoln, NE 68504-3467
www.iuniverse.com

The characters in this book are just that—characters—and not meant to depict any person, living or dead.

ISBN: 0-595-09703-0

Printed in the United States of America

For my mother
Mary Berrien Gamble Bartlett

Chapter 1

The fog horn on the jetty was braying like a demented jackass. Whole clusters of fog were attacking my eyes, playing havoc with my contacts, sending rivulets of condensation down my unruly hair and onto the back of my neck.

Down below the path the waves were pounding against the rocky cliffs in their relentless quest to take back the land which had erupted from the ocean's floor eons ago. It was high tide and occasionally spray from a gigantic wave added to my discomfort as salt water was added to the mix and the sharp tang of the salt got into my mouth.

A breeze picked up and began to thin the fog slightly. I could see a large mound of white further along. More solid than any fog, it was Misty Joy, my ever-present canine buddy. She is an Akita/Labrador mix. I call her an Akitador.

"Misty, come on. Let's get to the rink. It's colder out here than in there!" I could see her head come up as she quit sniffing whatever it is dogs sniff so diligently. She trotted back to me and we crossed the parking lot toward the building in front of us.

There were no cars in the lot, not surprising since it was only five A.M. Not too many years ago there would have been twenty or more vehicles sitting sullenly in the early morning mist. However, since school figures and their many permutations were declared *persona non grata* in international competitions, early morning patches are not the norm. A pity in a way, I had always liked doing figures, myself, but television audiences weren't interested in watching people go around in circles unless they were politicians. So, in a manner of speaking, it was "off with their heads."

In fact, it had been months since I had arrived at the rink at such an awful hour. Unfortunately, I had been saddled with the thankless task of producing the rink's first ice show. From concept to closing party would take about six months. Four production numbers, two precision teams and numerous solos, pairs and small group numbers meant a lot of work.

I had gotten the theme easily. *N'ice Shows*. That way we could use exhibition numbers already in progress and the precision teams' competition numbers. I had finished the music for three of the big production numbers and they were already in rehearsal. That left me with the final number plus odds and ends of octets and a few special solos.

For some reason I had woken up a couple of hours earlier with a Russian folk dance, *Kalinka*, running through my head. And there was the last production number. It would be a mixture of classical Russian composers and a sprinkling of their wonderful, quick folk dances. I wanted to get started recording it while no one was around.

The arena complex was only two years old and was designed for serious competitive skaters, the first new facility built in a number of years. On the Northern California Coast, just south of San Francisco, it had two Olympic size rinks and all the goodies skaters and their pros could want. An up-to-date music room with modern recording equipment was a great luxury. Many of the pros had donated their not-inconsiderable record collections to it. Compact discs are wonderful but long-play records are much easier to tape from. I knew I would find music I needed for the final number there.

Misty stood wagging her great plume of a tail at the main door, impatient to get in. One of her chief pleasures in life is to slide across the ice. We always have to make sure that all the gates to the ice surfaces are tightly closed. Otherwise her educated paws open one and off she goes. It is a great source of hilarity among the skaters privileged to watch her performances. She backs up a few steps to get a running start. As soon as the paws touch the ice they go in four different directions and she ends up sliding on her belly as she sails, inexorably, from one side of the rink to the other, ending with her nose touching the wooden railing at the far side.

"That's funny, Misty," I said as I started to put the key in the lock. "The door's open."

There were no lights on except the red EXIT signs along the corridor. A blinking red light on the telephone at the skate counter indicated that there were some messages on the voice mail. I stumbled over something in the doorway.

"Hello, anybody here?"

No one answered. The only sound was the hum of the refrigeration unit as it kicked on.

Misty wiggled her way past me and went on her hunt for access to the ice surface. She found one. She pushed the gate farther open with her nose and backed up. A short run, the sound of scrabbling paws and she was sailing on her way across the ice. A sudden thump caused me to look over to her. She had come to an unexpected stop in the middle of the rink. I could barely see her white fur, piled up against a dark mound of something.

A sharp woof, then a gentle crying sound came from her throat.

"Misty, what's the matter? It's only some of the kids playing a joke." The whimpering continued. That was not at all like her. "Oh, damn it, Misty. Okay, I'll come out and get you."

I hurried to the master light panel and switched the arena overhead lights on. Misty was still moaning softly, her head now resting on the dark thing on the ice. I stepped onto the ice gingerly in my tennis shoes. Unlike the dog, I had learned a long time ago that sliding across frozen water on my posterior wasn't much fun.

Misty tried to get up to come to me but couldn't get her feet under her. I moved cautiously towards the bundle. And stopped abruptly, skidding dangerously. Amid a pile of well-worn clothes was a curiously limp-looking arm, protruding from a ragged sleeve. Feet were visible poking below a pair of trousers. One foot was bare and blue-tinged under the dirt. The other one had an antique Doc Marten on. I leaned down and grabbed the bony wrist to check for a pulse. I saw the man's face. I had never seen him in my life. His hair was more grey than dark brown, almost white whiskers decorated the sunken-in face. The fingernails were broken, dirty, and looked as if they hadn't seen soap and water for years. A grimace on his face showed ill-kept teeth, some only broken-off stumps. A scruffy scarf that had once been a Royal Stewart design was wrapped loosely around his neck.

There was no pulse.

I grabbed Misty's collar and pulled her off the ice and headed for the office.

"Who's here? What's going on? What's that thing on the ice? Berrien, what are you doing here at this hour? I thought you only worked bankers' hours these days," rumbled a deep baritone voice with remnants of a French Canadian accent. It was the complex manager, Etienne Lepardieux. He had been a head-liner in the old *Ice Follies* for many years. For the past twenty years he had coached skaters and gradually moved into rink management. His job at *N'ice Skates* was ideal for him. There was an apartment on the second floor, complete with million dollar views of the Pacific Ocean. He had no family and this arrangement was perfect for him and for the arena. He was not simply close to the action but quite literally on top of it.

"'Tienne, we've got to call the Sheriff. That 'thing' on the ice is a dead body."

"Oh, come on, Berrien, that's not funny!" he said as he was getting ready to erupt in one of his monumental temper tantrums.

"I know it's not funny. It's a homeless person, I guess. No, 'Tienne, don't go over there," I said as he started out onto the ice. "The cops aren't going to be best pleased with all of the Misty hair, nor my handling his wrist. We'd better not go near him again."

He muttered something in his native French. I was sure that it was terribly impolite but my French vocabulary is severely limited. Etienne speaks excellent English except when he gets excited, which is fairly often, and then he lapses into his native tongue. He also still counts in French. Since he loves to work with the precision teams (no doubt that's why he was married to three different line skaters during his *Follies* days), their practices are often linguistically enhanced as he would count for the start, "Cinq, seis, sept, huit, GO!"

We headed for the office to make the call to the County Sheriff. He was still muttering, "Mon Dieu, mon Dieu!" We were both worried about the effect this event would have on the training center. Selfish? Definitely. But we had all been through a lot in getting this complex started and were just beginning to attract the big name skating coaches and their high profile students.

Miguel and Mishelle Andrade, former national pairs champions, and twins, had inherited the land from one of their father's uncles. It had, at one time, been a profitable truck farm and flower producer. Etienne, David Hockerby, myself and several other pros, some of whom were still skating in shows, had invested in the complex which we called *N'ice Skates*. For most of us our life's savings were in the project. It had been a long road from idea, to planning permission through a thicket of architects and engineers of various specialties to the live project. It still wasn't completed but we were on the way. The cottages for visiting pros and parents who wanted to stay with their child or children, a small infirmary, and a cafeteria where we would be able to monitor the skaters' diets effectively were all in the building or planning stages.

The spot was accessible to San Francisco International Airport and Half Moon Bay, the town just up the road, had a small airplane strip right off the Pacific Coast Highway. An ideal spot, close enough to civilization for ease of transportation and yet isolated enough for the serious skaters to be able to concentrate on skating without large crowds gathering to watch them practice.

The town itself was named Portugal, after the homeland of the original settlers. It and the surrounding farms had come upon hard times. The rise of the huge agribusinesses in California's Central Valley had cut serious inroads into the profitability of the small farmers on the Coast. About that same time the fishing had sunk to minimal catches. The residents were working harder than ever before for ever-decreasing profits.

The ice arena was bringing new life to the town. At this point, most of the skaters were from the Bay Area. They were either driven over the hills daily or had gotten rooms with the local residents. They went to the town school during non-practice times. We were also giving group lessons to the local kids. In fact, the main reason for the show was to let the skaters show off for their families and friends.

This death, from whatever causes, and however he came to be on the ice at five in the morning was going to mean notoriety for the rink. Etienne and I were both hoping that the old adage of any publicity being good publicity was true.

Chapter 2

The office was at least warm as we waited for the police to arrive.

"You wouldn't let me go see if I knew him, Berrien," complained Etienne. "Maybe I could have cleared up some questions if I had seen him."

"Do you know a lot of bums? This guy had broken-off teeth and his fingernails hadn't seen clippers in years. For that matter, I don't think any part of him had been washed for a month! He smelled awful."

We heard sirens in the distance and soon the wailing was right outside the front door. It sounded as though the entire coastside contingent was arriving along with an ambulance from Carmichael Hospital. It has always been a mystery to me why it was necessary for such noise for a dead person.

The racket died down. Etienne and I could see the revolving, blinking lights from all the emergency vehicles reflected in the main doors. We went out to the rink proper to greet the new arrivals.

A tall deputy came in first. The silver and blue uniform was as crisply fresh as though he hadn't been on duty all night. Polished boots reflected the revolving lights. His voice positively boomed as it echoed through the almost deserted building.

"Where's the body?"

I pointed to the mound of clothes out in the center of the rink, right on the red hockey circle.

"Oh, my God! How are we supposed to get out there?" the deputy almost howled.

A paramedic from the ambulance was gently pushing him aside. "Where's the victim? Let me see if I can do anything."

"No, he's dead. I checked for a pulse."

"What's he doing on the ice?"

"We don't even know who he is, let alone what he's doing out there, or how he got there. He only has one shoe on! The other is over by the door. I tripped over it when I came in," I offered, sounding slightly hysterical.

The deputy introduced himself. "I'm Sean Mather. Let's try to do things in order here. I need to ask a few questions while we're waiting for the doctor to check the victim. Now, who found the body?"

"I did. Well, actually, Misty Joy did."

"Okay. I want to talk to Misty Joy. Where is she? And you, sir, why are you here? For that matter, what are any of you doing here at this ridiculous hour?"

'Tienne and I both started to speak at once and the deputy held up his hand. "One at a time, please."

"I'm the manager, Etienne Lepardieux. I live here. There's an apartment upstairs. I saw the lights go on and came down to find Berrien here."

Oh, dear, he was even more upset than usual. He had just spouted the last sentences in French.

"Slow down. Can you speak English? Do you understand English?" asked the young law officer, enunciating each word slowly and carefully.

"Of course, I speak perfect English. Do you understand it yourself?" asked Etienne, completely oblivious to the fact that he had been rattling along in his native tongue.

The paramedic, having bravely slid out onto the ice to check the victim, came up to Deputy Mather. "He is most definitely dead. We'll have to call the coroner."

"How long has he been dead?"

"Can't tell. He's ice cold, of course. It's going to be a real problem. He doesn't look like he ate real regularly, either."

"All right. We'll have to wait for the coroner. We can't touch the body until he gets here." Mather turned to me again. "And where and who is the lady who found the stiff? I want to ask her some questions."

I looked around and found Misty asleep, as usual, with her nose aimed towards the secretary's candy drawer, and pointed to her. "You already have souvenirs of her on your trousers. I'm afraid she slid into him and you'll find her hair all over. She sheds her fur like a stripper sheds clothes. Oh, I'm Berrien Gamble, by the way."

"What's a dog doing on the ice? Oh, never mind. Did you touch the body?"

"Of course. His arm was kind of stuck out and I checked for a pulse. Left wrist, I think."

"Okay. It's only natural, I guess. Can either of you arrange some way for the coroner and the investigators to move around out there?"

We both thought for a moment. Then Etienne said, "Of course, the carpet we use for competition awards ceremonies. I'll go get it." He was, thankfully still back in English.

The deputy said, "No, you two—or three, as the case may be—stay here. One of my men will get it. Where is it?"

"Upstairs in the dance studio. It's in a closet to the right as you go in. It's pretty heavy."

Mather stuck his head out the door and bellowed, "Hey, Jack. Get in here. Bring Gus, too." Two big men marched in side by side, pulling both doors wide open.

'Tienne showed them to the stairway and gave directions to the dance studio. They clumped up the steps. We could hear their heavy boots in the upper hallway.

Voices were being raised outside. A high-pitched squeal, characteristic of Mrs. Taggert—one of the skating mothers—was the chief noisemaker. "What do you mean, we can't go in? Brandiwynne has a very important lesson scheduled at eight this morning. It's for her solo. Berrien said she'd have her music ready today! Now, out of my way!"

"Sorry, ma'am. You can't go in there. There's been an accident," rumbled another deputy.

"Accident? There's always accidents in an ice arena!" shrilled Mrs. Taggert. "What's that got to do with Brandiwynne's lesson? I want to see someone in charge here. Right now!"

I went to my skate bag and took out the tape I had made last night for Brandi, a short solo in the Oriental number. "May I just go out and give this to her? If she has the music, maybe she'll be quiet and go away. How long will we have to be closed or can we use the other ice surface today?"

"I don't have any idea how long this will take. The coroner will have to tell us. He should be here soon. We won't know what this guy died of until after the autopsy and coroner's report, anyhow. He could have just crawled in here to get warm and died," replied the deputy.

"Crawl into an ice arena to get warm? Ridiculous! Oh! I just remembered. The door was already open when I came in this morning. I thought it was strange then."

We could hear Mrs. Taggert still raising a fuss as Deputy Mather said, "Oh, go give that old bi___, er, lady, the tape so she leaves."

I stepped outside and was greeted by a veritable barrage of questions, not only from Juliet Taggert but several other skaters and their mothers or fathers.

David Hockerby, one of the other coach/owners, was also being held at bay by several deputies. "Berrien, what the hell is going on here?"

"Hold on, David. Let me give this music to Brandi."

Finding mother and daughter easily by sound, I hurried over. "Here, Brandi. I want you to take this home and listen to it. There's fifteen seconds of the part before your solo and it ends right at the last note of your number. Think about it and see if you can put a program together. Then we'll work on it together."

"What about Brandiwynne's lesson this morning? Isn't she going to get it?" whined Juliet. "I demand to know why all these officers are here. You must tell me! We all need to know what's going on. We may need to get psychologists to help our children deal with the trauma."

"Look," I said, "why don't you all get the kids to school now and give us a call before this afternoon's session? Things will be clearer by then."

At this novel suggestion—that the skaters go to school at a normal time instead of filtering in after their morning practices—the parents looked dumbfounded and the kids glared at me with distinctly rebellious eyes. I wasn't too sure that the school was going to be terribly pleased either. The influx of young school-age children had revitalized Portugal's small school. There were now enough students to keep the classrooms open instead of having to bus the local children to near-by Half Moon Bay. That was one of the selling points that had gotten us the permission to build the complex. But having this crew arrive more than two hours earlier than usual was going to put some noses out of joint, for sure.

Deputy Mather, who was standing at the open doors, heartily endorsed the idea. "Yeah, all you kids go to school. Ms. Gamble, come on back in. We'll start with some basic questions. I don't know what's holding up the coroner and the lab boys."

"Can David come in? He's one of the owners, too."

"Sure, why not. Just as far as the office, though."

Grumbling, the parents hoisted the heavy skate bags to their shoulders and trooped back to their cars, accompanied by their equally disgruntled progeny.

Well, why should they have a good day when mine had started out so nastily?

CHAPTER 3

The scenes of crime team had just arrived and were studiously looking everywhere but the ice. Doorknobs, metal railings and wooden boards were being decorated with a fine, sullen-colored powder, the better to locate fingerprints. I wished them luck. There must be thousands of them.

Finally, the white van with the legend *San Mateo County Coroner* painted discretely on the door drew up outside. The coroner's assistant hopped out of the driver's side, clutching an old-fashioned doctor's satchel.

"I'm Dr. Carmody. Where's the body?" He was a short, scraggly little man who didn't look old enough to have graduated from the Kiddie Korner Kindergarten much less medical school.

We all pointed in unison toward the center of the ice.

"Oh, shit! How are we supposed to work out there? No one ever told me that I had to take ice skating lessons to be a pathologist."

Since David, Etienne and I were not sure of the proper protocol, we stood silently while the accumulated majesty of the law contemplated the problem.

Jack and Gus had deposited the three heavy rolls of red, outdoor carpet in a pile at the edge of the rink. Sitting there it sure wasn't giving anyone any help. Finally, I said, "Suppose we three get our skates on and lay the carpet out around the body? That ought to get you started. The blades will leave marks on the ice and so will the carpet but you'll be able to tell the skate marks from shoe prints, or bare feet for that matter. The ice was resurfaced before this guy landed here. That's the best I can suggest."

Dr. Carmody looked marginally relieved although he was clearly not looking forward to crawling around the ice, carpeted or not. "Okay, let's try it that way. At least we can get some pictures and I can examine the body superficially anyhow."

Soon we had wrestled one roll from the gate to the corpse. Then we started to pull the next one out.

"Stop! Let me go out there now and get as many photos as I can before you lay the other two rolls." The good doctor stepped gingerly onto the bright red plastic rug.

"It's all right. You can't skate on it," Etienne called out. That might be true but in our time we had all seen some Very Important People in the world of figure skating sliding on their altogether too ample posteriors in scenarios being televised to the world while navigating on the treacherous stuff.

The bright light of the flash attachment to the camera spluttered as Dr. Carmody clicked off frame after frame. Then he knelt down and carefully checked the body. "I don't see any evidence of any injuries. He probably froze to death out here. All right, bring out the rest of the carpets. Right around the body, but try not to mess anything up. This is all most unusual, to say nothing of downright illegal, even, maybe."

With those ominous words, David, Etienne and I hauled more carpet out onto the ice and tried to circle the corpse with the unyielding, unwieldy stuff. Cameras were still clicking away rapidly. I hated to think of the pictures the cameraman was getting of my own nether regions, as we fought with the carpet. It was finally placed to Dr. Carmody's satisfaction and we skated to the side of the rink.

By this time the coroner was well into the routine. He had bagged the hands and feet, taken the body temperature—which was sure going to be a first in coastal California for low temperature—and was going through the raggedy pockets searching for some kind of identification.

Mather gathered Etienne, David and me into the office. Misty Joy was still there, snoring loudly. "Okay, let me get some idea of the routine here. Ms. Gamble, why were you here so early?"

I explained about the show and the music. I'm afraid I made rather a production of the processes necessary to put on a show. My nerves were definitely beginning to fray. The deputy's eyes were glazing over as I finished. It really must be the pits to get a call to a dead body at the end of a twelve hour shift!

"I know this is a stupid question but why was the dog on the ice?"

More explanations followed.

"When was the ice last made? Do you guys have one of those noisy things like they use at hockey games to make ice?"

The clod was referring to our *magic monsters!* We were all three old enough to remember making ice with snow shovels, squeegees and a garden hose. We decided to take umbrage at the same moment.

'Tienne started off, again in French, "You mean a Zamboni? We have three! All kept in perfect running order."

I said, "Of course we do. Three of them and they all work."

David commented rather more laconically, "Naturally we do. You can't run a rink without them these days."

Realizing that he had somehow insulted us beyond all reason, Mather said, "Okay, okay. Didn't mean to put your rink down. Now when was the ice made? Who made it? Obviously, your unwanted guest wasn't there then."

Etienne, a notorious insomniac, said, "I heard the Zamboni running about one o'clock this morning. Miki and Sheli were working with their new pair team, Paul and Tami, on lifts out on the ice late last night. Miki probably ran the thing himself."

"What's his number? I'll call him now. Ask him to come over here," muttered Mather, more to himself than to us.

"Sure, the number's on the speed dial, number four, I think."

The deputy dialed the twins' home number. We could hear the phone ringing on the other end. Finally, someone picked up the receiver. Mather carefully identified himself, telling whichever one of the two had answered the phone where he was, but not why he was calling.

"Mr. Andrade, can you and your sister come down to the rink, please?"

Silence on our end while Miki asked a question.

"Yes, now. It's important."

Another short silence.

"No, I can't tell you what it's about. We'll talk when you get down here."

He turned back to us as he hung up the phone. "Mr. Andrade and his sister are on their way, or will be as soon as they get dressed."

We heard a loud shout just then and the unmistakable, sickening sound of someone's head hitting the ice. It was just like the noise a watermelon makes after it falls off the back of a truck and hits the macadam road. We all looked out the office door. One of the coroner's assistants had slipped and fallen.

Long years of tending to friends and students caused 'Tienne, David and me to leap up and head for the ice, Mather trailing behind us.

"Don't go out there. Dr. Carmody's there. He can take care of him."

We slid to a stop, me with one foot dangling out over the ice, graceful as always.

The doctor went to check on his assistant who was struggling to sit up. His hands, clad in their thin surgical gloves, kept slipping backwards. Even from where we were, we could see a thin trickle of blood running from his receding hairline down onto his cheek.

Carmody got to him and examined him briefly. "He'll be okay," he shouted. "Just get one of the skaters out here to help him up. We'll take him to the emergency room when we leave, just to be sure."

David skated over and lifted the frightened but essentially uninjured man up, and helped him back onto the carpet.

After a few more minutes Dr. Carmody requested that a body bag be brought out to him. "I'll have to wait until we do the autopsy. There doesn't seem to be a mark on him from what I can see here. But I can't straighten him out."

A stretcher was brought in from the coroner's van. The sad, frozen bundle that had just recently been a living man was bagged, labeled and carried out of the arena.

CHAPTER 4

The tires of the retreating van screeched to a halt to avoid the ocean blue jeep Grand Cherokee, with the white *N'ice Skates* legend superimposed over a graceful California Juniper on the door. as it squealed around the drive towards the entrance to the complex. The Andrade twins had arrived, Sheli driving while Miki tried to use a battery-operated shaver. The two skaters have raven black hair, complete with the bluish sheen that so often accompanies such a rich color. As a result, Miki also has a black beard almost twenty-four hours a day. It is a constant battle for him to remain clean-shaven.

Sheli was munching on a quickly toasted muffin, dripping with butter and her favorite blueberry jam. They tumbled hastily out of the car and headed for the rink at a brisk gallop.

"What's going on? Why are all these police cars around here? What happened?" mumbled Sheli around the last bite of muffin.

"Oh, God! What's gone wrong now?" This question was from the now clean-shaven Miki.

Deputy Mather stepped forward and introduced himself. "There's been an accident of sorts. I need to ask you a couple of questions. Come in to the office where we can talk. We don't want traffic to slow down more than it already is."

I looked outside. Sure enough, the cars on the Pacific Coast Highway were traveling at the proverbial snail's pace, gawking at the collection of county cars parked every which way in the rink's parking lot. Some, no doubt, were complaining to their carpool buddies about the trouble they had predicted the rink would bring with it.

Now there were six of us, well, seven if you counted the gentle giant still sprawled on the floor, paws making running motions, dreaming of chasing a deer or even a rabbit. The front office was not designed to hold so many people.

Etienne turned to the deputy. "Would you like to use my office?" he asked as he gestured towards the closed door to his right. "It's a lot bigger than this. We have our coaches' meetings in there every week. You'd be more comfortable."

David and I exchanged glances. We knew that 'Tienne was longing to get in there to the bottle that was in the bottom desk drawer. His eyes were still bloodshot from last night's drinks. He usually didn't start this early in the morning but the strain was beginning to tell on him.

"Oh, thanks. That's a great idea. But let me get the lab boys to check it out first to make sure we don't miss anything. Hey, Russ," he roared out the door, "get in here and check out this other room here. We need to use it."

Russ slapped his hands on his trousers, raising a billow of powdery fingerprint dust. I wasn't sure whether it was to get his hands clean or get some of the mess off the silver grey trousers. Whichever it was, it didn't work and he arrived in the office still snowing greyish-black powder.

Etienne reached in his pocket and pulled out his set of keys. There were so many he must have been working out in the weight room to be able to carry them around without listing to starboard.

Selecting the key to his office he was starting to open the door when Russ yelled, "Hold it. I'd better check that for prints first."

After the ritual, 'Tienne opened the door and Russ, Sean Mather and he went in. David, Miki, Sheli and I remained in the secretary's room with Misty while the big room was gone over thoroughly. It obviously hadn't been broken in to and there was no chaotic mess around the desk or the file cabinets.

When the fingerprint man left, we joined the group in 'Tienne's office. He had made coffee while the room was being inspected. It smelled wonderful. I had had one cup of instant coffee at home along with a slice of almost toast—I say almost because my toaster never wants to let the bread turn brown so it just gets dry. A quick check of the ornate clock that held pride of place on Etienne's desk showed that it was already ten o'clock! Five hours since we had found the body.

Miki and Sheli were still mystified. Miki, never known for his patience, finally stamped his foot. "What the hell has happened? Why are the police here?" he asked as his voice rose in volume with each word.

"Ms. Gamble found a body out on the ice," answered Deputy Mather. "Did you make the ice last night? What time did you all leave?"

"A body? Who's body? Yes, yes, I made the ice last night, about, oh, I guess, one or maybe one thirty."

"Did you and your sister leave before or after your skaters?"

Sheli piped up, "I watched them get in the car and start off while Miki was running the Zamboni. Our Jeep was the only car in the lot when we went out."

"Did you lock the rink up? In particular, the front door?"

"Of course we did. I checked the door myself," said Miki, his voice now its usual smooth tenor.

"Now, Ms. Gamble, you said the door was unlocked when you got here, didn't you?"

"It was, yes. Actually it was partially open. I tripped over that old shoe."

David, up until now mostly silent, spoke. "If Miki locked up, then how did the dead man get in here? And why? We don't keep much money around. Most of our charges are billed to the parents monthly. Even the public session cash gets deposited every night. You did deposit the money last night, didn't you, 'Tienne?"

"Of course I did. Took it into the night deposit at nine o'clock in Half Moon Bay."

Mather decided that he had gotten all the help we could give him. Now, he had reports to write and evidence to take to the lab. For that he had a long drive over the coastal mountains to headquarters in Redwood City. Then it would be, hopefully, to bed for some sleep before his next shift started.

"Okay, people. You can use the other ice surface after Noon. Don't let anyone on this one 'til you hear from me." He was yawning widely as he walked out into the now sunny day.

Soon the remainder of the troops trickled away with further instructions not to disturb the ice.

"Hey, wait!" Etienne yelled. "Can we at least pick up the carpet? That's going to ruin the ice underneath it if we don't get it up soon. That's an expensive proposition to tear the whole surface down and start over, to say nothing of losing several days of ice time."

"Yeah, sure. That's okay. We got the pictures. But don't use that noisy machine on it quite yet," answered our friend, Russ.

We all sat with our now-cold coffee, unanswered questions running around in circles in all our heads. We got down to work and rescheduled patches for the lower level skaters and added two skaters per freestyle session for the upper levels. It would work for a couple of days.

Finally, I left the gathering and went out to the music room to find *Kalinka* and the rest of the music for the production number.

I had just about finished the taping when David stuck his head in the door.

"Berrien, what's really going on?"

"Oh, shit!" I swore. He had startled me and I missed the ending I wanted. "David, hold on a couple of minutes. Come on in. This number has to be done today! I'm sick of this. My fingers are bleeding from pushing buttons, and I'm cross-eyed from this stupid stop-watch."

He came into the room and sat down on one of the leather couches. David is a former National and International ice dance champion with his late wife. Marlene had died tragically in a plane accident while she was traveling with several competitors to Pacific Coast Championships two years ago. He had been devastated and is still subject to what we politely call his moods.

His carriage is superb. When he walks, it is like watching a ballroom dancer float across the floor. He sits like that, too, back absolutely straight but not rigid. There is a fluidity to all his movements that belies his 50 years.

David is still a handsome man, eyes the bright blue of a California summer sky, hair now more grey than the auburn of his youth, slim build without a hint of a paunch. I had known him a long time. We had met, not through skating but at a college fraternity party. And even after all these years I still don't know what he thinks or feels. He is a most self-contained person.

His greatest talent lay in his teaching. Where many pros threw temper tantrums when their skaters weren't performing their best, David always kept calm. He practiced sports psychology counseling long before there was ever such a specialty. And his skaters love him for it. They win a lot of titles, too.

The gift of silence is also one of his blessings. He sat contentedly while I fussed and fiddled with the last piece for the Russian number. Finally, I was satisfied with the ending.

"David, listen to this music. See if you like it." I started the tape from the beginning. The soul of Russia could be heard in the opening music, sad, heavy and then slowly gaining momentum as the classical music was replaced by the peasant dances so well used by Rodnina and Zeitsev in their wonderful reign as Pair Champions of just about everything. The number timed out at 12 minutes. Just right.

While listening, David's feet had begun to tap out rhythms, soon he was up moving around the room, improvising steps, visualizing the choreography already.

"That's marvelous, Berrien. It'll be great. I'll help you do the number on the ice."

That was good news. So far, the offers of help from the other pros for anything other than their students' solos had been so rare as to be non-existent. If David started to work, the others would insist on doing a number, too. Competitors never die, they just teach!

"Wonderful, David. We'll have fun!"

I rewound the tape and shoved a blank one in the dubbing side to make a copy. After that was done, David and I went back to the main office.

Gillian Tower, our secretary, had finally been allowed to come in. She was busy phoning skaters and parents with the rescheduled sessions. Not a job I would relish at all.

"Have you gotten Mrs. Taggert yet? I might as well do Brandi's number this afternoon. I'll write it down for her, too."

"Yes," Gillian answered, "they'll be here at three this afternoon. Mrs. Taggert expects an hour lesson, though. She said to tell you that it was the least you could do to make up for the mix-up this morning."

Etienne was still stalking around, glowering. David asked, "Have you had lunch yet?"

"No," 'Tienne spit out. "Do you expect me to eat when such horrible things happen in *my* rink?"

"You need to. Come on. Berrien and I are going to the *Boat Dock* and treat ourselves to some of that crab bisque. You come, too."

We watched Etienne. He has a wonderfully expressive face. Dark brown eyes which could scare the dickens out of a poor skate guard or soothe a child who had fallen and was frightened. His smile is an indication of how he was feeling. If it is wolfish, watch out. He is not handsome but has that French *savoir faire* that made his looks secondary to his powerful personality. He still smoked. Three packs a day. His voice is always hoarse, and during rehearsals he frequently loses it from shouting so much—into a walkie talkie! My eardrums have often been the target of his sarcastic remarks made at a decibel level well above that of a major rock concert.

Tall for a skater, he had made a wonderful adagio pair team with his successive tiny wives. They invented several moves that brought screams to the audiences' throats every night. Throw moves not allowed in any amateur competition were right up his alley. Given his disposition I'd bet that his wife of the year never fought with him before a performance.

Both David and I had known him for years. He was having a hard time coping with the death of a stranger right under his nose.

"Okay. That sounds good. They make a decent soup."

That is high praise indeed coming from Etienne whose cooking skills are legendary. Invitations to his annual Christmas parties for a hundred of his closest friends are much sought after. He does all the cooking himself, starting in July with the freezable things. The real goodies are his meat pies, which are made from his mother's recipe, which he guards jealously.

"By the way, where are Miki and Sheli?" I asked, hoping to make a big party at the restaurant so we would be sure to get a table by the window so we could watch the ocean.

"The deputy asked them to go see if they knew who the dead man is. I have to go over later today, too. That's your fault, Berrien. If you'd let me look this morning, I wouldn't have to make that awful trip."

"Well, the deputy could have had you look earlier, this morning. Don't blame me!"

"Children, children," sighed David, well accustomed to settling the two of us down, "don't fight. Let's go get lunch."

CHAPTER 5

Lunch had been served. The crab bisque was as good as ever but we were not eating it with much enthusiasm. I concentrated on crumbling pieces of still-warm French bread into even smaller pieces. We stared gloomily out the window. The birds were darting in and out of the waves, eagerly in search of their lunch with much more energy than we were putting into our soup. We had had to put up with questions from our waiter and from the chef/owner of the restaurant. They had been among the cars tied up in the traffic this morning and wanted a first hand account of the excitement. We had given them a short version so that they would leave us alone.

'Tienne was still sulking about having to drive over to the coroner's in the afternoon. David was always quiet. And I was thinking of my hour lesson with Brandi and, of course, Mrs. Taggert.

Brandi was a nice kid. By some process that I would never comprehend, she was a polite, quiet child who worked hard at her skating. The problem, besides the obvious one of Juliet Taggert, was that she didn't have that spark that radiates from the truly talented in any area. Her mother was a frustrated actress who had appeared in small parts in several "B movies" and equally uninspiring television shows. She had decided when Brandi was born that Brandi would be a *star*. Since she had been watching the World Figure Skating Championships when she went into labor, she was convinced that her child was destined to amaze the world of skating.

Skating mothers were always a trial. Mrs. Taggert was a whole judge's yearly calendar of them! No amount of explaining to her that Brandi was not a candidate for a national title dampened Juliet's enthusiasm for the child's lessons. Nor did Brandi's workman-like but unexciting performances at competitions.

The young girl had been named with stardom in mind. Brandiwynne Taggert. Her mother dressed her in custom-made skating outfits. Even the practice dresses were weighed down with sequins and bugle beads. Her mouse brown hair was always pulled back tightly. A thin veil of bangs drooped despondently on her forehead. The bun was covered in more beads matching the outfit of the day.

The hairstyle, unfortunately, only served to emphasize her face. It would have looked more at home on a Tennessee Walking horse. Needless to say, the poor child was laughed at behind her back. Her fellow skaters had nicknamed her *Whinny*.

I had given her a solo in the Oriental number to make her feel good. And I was sure that she would do a good job of the number. It was only a short one, but would improve her presentation, I hoped. It sometimes is a big help if a performer gets to simply perform instead of compete. Feelings come out better then and I was hoping that this would happen with Brandi.

Three o'clock did arrive along with the Taggerts. Juliet, dragging her morning mink coat, was in good voice. "Honestly, how could you let someone die in here? Don't you understand that the children are going to be traumatized? I, myself, will not sleep a wink tonight. What is this town coming to when a bum can come into an ice arena and die?"

I wasn't sure whether she really expected an answer but that last statement was just too much! "I can assure you, Mrs. Taggert, that we will strive to do our best to prevent a repeat performance. It wasn't in our five year plan. Brandi, get your skates on so we can start your new number."

We got out onto the ice and both stroked around, getting the feel of the cold surface and warming up. Brandi did a few simple jumps and spins and we started on her solo. I held a portable tape player and we worked on the moves that would suit the music and her style. She picked up the idea quickly and even came up with some steps of her own that would do nicely. The hour went well and the whole program was ready.

Feeling we had accomplished a lot we skated to the side and got off the ice. Oops, too close to Mrs. Taggert. "Is that all she is going to do in that number? She has to have a longer piece! I have ordered her costume and it's a very expensive one. Solidly beaded. I want her to have more to do so that the dress will show up."

"Mrs. Taggert, I hope you can cancel the order for the dress until I see the design. I told you that I wanted approval of every costume in this show. I have the designs in my head and none are solidly beaded."

"Well, I just want Brandi to look her best. We can afford the most elegant things, you know."

"Look, we want everyone to look their best, and skate their best, but this number is not going to be about beading. A lot of gold braid and red and black satin, yes, but not a load of sequins! Please let me do my job!"

Locking horns with Mrs. Taggert was the last thing I needed to do. It hadn't started out as a good day and was rapidly running downhill. I glanced up as the front door opened. A giant smile creased my face, and incidentally revealed all the wrinkles age, too much stage make-up and smoking were leaving on my skin.

Marguerita Freitas had come in, loaded on one side with her school book bag and dragging her skating paraphernalia in a wheeled luggage container on the other. She was my pride, joy and sometimes despair.

When the rink first opened we had offered a free series of class lessons to all the children in town. The idea was to introduce the sport to a population who had, mostly, only seen elite skaters on television. We wanted to cement a good relationship with the town of Portugal while adding to the local skating population. Our hope was that a short course in how to skate would encourage the kids to spend their Friday or Saturday nights with us, while we prayed that instilling some basic knowledge would make them safer skaters.

The program had been a wild success. Almost every child had taken the first series of classes. The parents, many of whom had opposed the complex, were disarmed and had finally agreed that our new business was a welcome addition to the town. Several of the kids had continued into the more advanced classes. Marguerita was the prize.

She had stepped onto the ice the first day of class as if she had been born wearing skates. A true natural. There are more of them than one might think. The real test, though, is not just innate talent but desire, too. One without the other dooms everyone involved to serious frustration. Marguerita had both, talent and desire.

Her parents were very protective of her. She had been a sickly child, catching everything and anything that came along. A much loved only daughter who had four older brothers, all in their teens and early twenties when she came along. Rodrigo, her father, watched out for her vigilantly, ever careful that the frivolous side of skating not catch her—or him—unaware.

Rodrigo, in fact, had been a major thorn in our side when we were still in the development of the arena. He, along with many others, had worried about the effects that so many strangers would have on the old town. He had organized petitions against the project and even written letters to Miki and Sheli begging them not to use their land for such a useless purpose. Because of these activities, he was always shy when he brought Marguerita in, not ashamed but abashed to find his daughter a major player in the arena that he had so opposed.

In two short years she had passed the first four figure tests, preliminary, first, second and third. With the end of required figures in international competition now a reality, she only had one more that she absolutely had to pass. She was working hard on those figures and should finish it within a month or so.

Marguerita was already a beauty at eleven and was only going to get more lovely as the years went by. Her hair is a bittersweet chocolate-colored brown, with eyes to match. The eyes are so enormous that they seem to be the only feature in her face. Until she smiles. Then the generous mouth splits into a huge grin of sheer joy. She wears that grin almost all the time she is on the ice, except when she makes a mistake or falls. Then the smile fades while she tries to figure out what she has done wrong to cause the mishap.

As an antidote to Brandi and Mrs. Taggert, they were a welcome sight. Had I had a moment to think, I would have worried that the family would keep Marguerita away.

While she was putting on her skates and doing her warm-up exercises, I went into the office to check on Misty Joy. Gillian assured me that the dog was doing fine. I couldn't have told if she had even moved, the pink and black nose was still pointed at the candy drawer where Gillian always kept proper doggie treats, too.

"Hello, Rodrigo. I'm glad to see you both here today."

"Yes. I heard there was some trouble here this morning. What happened? Is it safe for Marguerita?"

"We don't know what really happened. I found a dead man out on the ice early this morning. He didn't have any identification and looked like he was really down on his luck. Etienne, Miki and Sheli are over in Redwood City to see if they can identify him. I sure couldn't. We don't even know how he died but I'm sure there's no danger to any of the skaters. But we've hired new security guards for the night time, anyhow."

"Good. Delores and I don't want anything to happen to our baby girl."

"No, of course you don't. Nor do I, Rodrigo. She's someone special and I'm not just talking about her skating, either."

"Okay, 'Rita, time to skate. Do your five laps first." I glanced over into the stands. Mrs. Taggert was watching closely. I surely did hope that they weren't going to stay. We were going to start work on Marguerita's show solo. Hers was a *cold spot*, not out of one of the production numbers, which was not going to please Juliet at all!

I was using a perennial favorite of skaters, *Malaguena* to showcase her delicate Latin beauty. The version I had taped was one I had never heard used before—a guitar solo by Roy Clark. He had taken the stately music and played it as a fiery paso doble. It had been hard to cut it to two minutes and thirty seconds, it was all so wonderful. As it was, the poor kid was going to have to go into serious training just to last that shorter time!

That hour passed quickly. The music sounded wonderful on the arena sound system and we got most of the program blocked out. Refinements of arm and head movements would come later. 'Rita went on skating as I headed off the ice.

Brandi and her mother were gone, thank goodness. One more run in with that particular skating mother would have sent me running to Etienne's stock in his lower desk drawer.

"Is it okay if I use the music system now?" called David. He had been working with one of his dance teams. "Tests are next week and this Blues is going to be very blue if we don't get to work with the music!"

"Oh, sure, I'm sorry, I didn't mean to hog the equipment. I've had it. Misty Joy and I are headed home. At least Philip is out of town again so I don't even have to think about cooking." Philip is my phantom husband. He works as an engineering consultant and is gone more than he is home. We had so much in the way of frequent flyer mileage that we could go around the world first class. The only problem is that we are never together long enough to plan the trip.

As I put my head in the door of the office to call the dog, Miki and Sheli burst into the rink.

"We identified him! At least we think so," Sheli announced. "It's one of Mom's brothers. We haven't seen him for years and of course he didn't look like a bum then. Mom's going to be shocked. We've got to call her now. I guess she'll come down from Sea Ranch to see if it is really Uncle Tomaso."

Gillian had gone to the ladies room and Sheli was on the phone to her mother. I overheard her say, "Can you come down tonight?" Then another phone line lit up. Etienne was in his office talking to the reporter/errand girl from the *Portugal Post*, our local weekly paper, so I picked up the phone at the skate counter.

"*N'ice Skates*. May I help you?"

"Hi, Berrien. It's Paul Light. Is Tami there, by any chance?"

"No, Paul. I haven't seen her all day. Did you take her all the way home last night? Have the police called you?"

"I just got in from work. Haven't even listened to my messages on the machine. Tami and I are supposed to work with Miki and Sheli in the dance studio tonight but I called her apartment and don't get any answer. Do you suppose she's sick? She was okay last night when I dropped her off. Why in the world would the police be calling me? Did something happen to Tami?"

"No, as far as I know Tami's all right. It's just that we had a bit of a problem here this morning. Actually, I found a dead man on the ice when I got here. We've had practically the entire Sheriff's office around here all day. Deputy Mather is probably trying to see you and Tami because of the time you left here last night. Maybe she's being interviewed now. Check your messages and call us back."

Sheli was still talking to her mother. "No, Mom. Miki can't fly up tonight and get you. The fog's already almost on the ground here and I bet it's just as bad up at Sea Ranch." Silence on our end while Mrs. Andrade had her say.

"Mom, go look out the window. You don't need to watch the weather forecast on the television!" Another silence.

"Mother!" wailed Sheli in exasperation, "Miki's not going to fly up in this fog. We don't have a tower here and the strip at Sea Ranch is dangerous on a sunny, calm day! If you don't want to drive down now, wait until morning and we'll see what the weather is then."

Sheli hung up the phone, or to be accurate she slammed it down hard. The twins' mother had been a skating mother almost on a par with Mrs. Taggert. Her battles with a succession of coaches were legendary and she was obviously still trying to dominate her grown-up off-spring.

"Did you tell her what happened?"

"Yes. She says she probably wouldn't recognize Uncle Tomaso herself, it's been so long. But she'll come down tomorrow, anyhow. I hope she drives herself. That way, at least, one of us won't have to chauffeur her around all the county."

"Did you learn any more about how he died or how he got into the rink when you were at the coroner's place?"

"No, not really. But I did hear a deputy tell another one that the shoe by the door matched the one he was wearing. And they found an empty cream sherry bottle in the dumpster out the back with two sets of fingerprints on it. Wonder if that means anything?"

"The empty wine bottle probably doesn't have anything to do with it but I wonder how the shoes got separated. Sheli, Paul is looking for Tami. Have you or Miki seen her today?"

"Mmmm…no. But they have an off-ice lift lesson tonight at six."

The phone rang again. Gillian had, by now, swept her desk clean and gone home to her two toddlers and their father. The *Portugal Post* reporter was still with Etienne so I picked it up. Before I could even get a greeting out Paul was talking.

"Berrien, what should I do? Tami's missing!"

"What do you mean, 'missing'?" I shouted. Sheli's head snapped around and she mouthed "Is that Paul?" I nodded yes and she raced into the office to get in on the call.

"Hold on, Paul. Sheli's getting on the line, too. How do you know she's missing?"

"I listened to my messages. You were right. The police do want to talk to us. They called three times today. Then I got worried that Tami wasn't answering her phone so I came over to her place. She's not here and there's a note tacked on her door. It says she'll call me sometime this evening or tomorrow morning. She's going to miss our practice! What the hell is going on? She's *never* done anything like this before."

Sheli broke into the conversation. "Paul, don't touch the note. Just leave it there and come over to the rink. We'll think of something."

"Paul, have you called Tami's parents? She might have gotten a 'rush home' message from them," I asked. Then I turned to Sheli. "I'm going home. Misty needs to eat. I think maybe when Paul gets here you had better call the Sheriff. Something's not right and it wouldn't be a good idea to hold out on the police. Call me when you know what Tami's parents said to Paul. Oh, and tell Etienne about this latest mystery, but not until after *the press* leaves!"

I called for Misty Joy. She awoke from her slumbers and ambled over to me. She is always amiable and anxious to please.

We walked out into the fog again, although Sheli had exaggerated the thickness of it. What a day! Six o'clock at night and I had hardly sat down all day except for that long-ago lunch. My back was howling its fury at such neglect. Skaters, particularly those of us who got involved in the sport before cross-training was even thought of, have unhealthy backs. Years of pounding from jump landings, both those successfully landed on the blade and those less successfully landed on other portions of the anatomy, plus the extreme back arch expected at the end of each move took its toll on all of us. I wished now that I had driven in the morning. I wasn't looking forward to the mile-long hike.

Misty bounded along the path, exploring all the new smells that had accumulated since she had last checked out the area. It was high tide again and the crashing waves just suited my own tumultuous mood.

Oh, well, at least I had gotten the last production number recorded so we could start those rehearsals next week. It would be fun to work with David on the footwork that he had been playing with in the record library.

The dog bounded up the steps to the house. I followed at a slower pace, after all, I had been working while she snoozed all day.

As always, I paused to admire the home that Philip and I had designed together with the help of the architect for the arena complex. It is set back from the cliff overlooking the Pacific Ocean far enough to practically insure that it won't be gobbled up by a hungry ocean in some unimaginable storm. But it is close enough to have an incredible view from all the rooms. Of course, in the event of a serious earthquake, we might find ourselves on a small island somewhat to the west of Nevada. Essentially, if the house were in Charleston, South Carolina, it would be called a shotgun house. One room wide with a hallway reaching the entire length of the place except for the two end rooms, the master bedroom and the family room. We are proud of it and enjoy living in it.

The phone was ringing as I opened the door. I let the answering machine pick up the call. I was in no frame of mind to talk to anyone.

"Berrien, it's Etienne. Pick up the phone." A pause, then, "Damn it, I know you're there. Get the phone!" This last statement was more of a demand than a request.

"Yes, 'Tienne. What now?"

"Have you heard this latest outrage?"

"What outrage?"

"Tami Tompson is missing."

"Yes, I was there when Paul called. Has he gotten to the rink yet? He's supposed to see Sheli."

"He came in about five minutes ago. Sheli says you think we ought to tell the cops about it."

"I do. What with a dead body in the rink and now a missing skater we can't keep anything from them. Did Paul call Tami's parents?"

"He's doing it right now."

"I'll hang on until you find out what they say."

"Berrien, Paul doesn't get any answer at the Tompsons," howled Etienne.

"Then call the police. Now."

"I'll let you know what happens."

"Unless you find out something definite, don't call tonight!" I turned the bell off so I wouldn't hear any more calls and went to feed the dog.

Chapter 6

The white, furry face, flavored with doggie breath, was close to mine as I woke up to a bright, sunshiny day. Misty's pink tongue was washing my face as she tried to get me up and moving. She seemed to be saying, "Oh, come on, Mom. We've got places to go and things to do."

A groan escaped from my throat as I remembered yesterday. Had Tami been found, I wondered.

There was nothing to do but roll from underneath the cozy, warm comforter and go places, wherever they might take us. I fumbled around for my robe and hauled it on while the dog bounced around joyfully. We found our way to the kitchen and I put some hazelnut coffee in the pot. While waiting for the pot to finish dripping, I checked the answering machine for messages, remembering to turn the ringer back on.

There were seven calls!

"Hello, Berrien. This is Juliet Taggert." *Oh, wonderful!* "I just wanted to make sure that you were cutting the longer number that we discussed for Brandi. I really do want her to show up well in her new costume. Well, I'll see you tomorrow."

"Berrien, it's Etienne. Answer the damn phone! Paul couldn't reach Tami's mom and dad tonight. He said he'll try later when he gets home. In the meantime, we're putting off notifying the police."

I didn't think I could stand anymore good news until the coffee was ready.

"Hi, honey. I just thought I'd call to talk to you. Guess you're not home yet. The meetings went really great today so I'll probably be home a day earlier than we thought. G'dey." That was Philip, calling from Sydney, Australia for a chat. He always picks up a local phrase and uses it repeatedly until the next trip to somewhere new.

"Hey, Berrien, I couldn't get Tami's parents. I'll try in the morning." *Paul, what happened to later in the evening?*

"Berrien, it's Sheli. Miki and I are really worried about Tami. Can we come over? Berrien, pick up the phone. Please pick up the phone."

The coffee was finally finished dribbling into the carafe. I lunged for it before the next message could start. What I really was wondering was who had died and left me as den mother.

"Berrien, it's Etienne again. It's eight in the morning. Where are you? Or did you disappear too? Aren't you coming in today? Call me!" *Yes, milord.*

Finally, coffee and the last message. "Hello. Here is Mr. Gomarch. I'm sorry to be calling you but your cousin gave you as a reference. He's been in an accident and we need information. Can you please call me at 809-555-1212? Thank you. I look forward to your call."

Wonderful. That was all I needed. I had just been reading about that phone scam in the Sunday paper. Well, that was one call that didn't need to be returned.

I let Misty Joy outside for her morning necessities. Philip and I had discussed a doggy door but it would have had to be so big that a linebacker for the Raiders would have fit through it. A few minutes later she was standing at the door waiting to come in for a morning snack before our travels. A bagel, scrounged from the freezer, was toasting. She could share that.

A quick shower for me and off we went, driving this time. I had debated returning those calls, but decided against it. We'd just head for the rink and talk in person.

The day was one of those special gifts that bring sunshine and warm, light breezes to the Coast in early Spring. The fog had retreated beyond the horizon. The sun was making the waves glitter as if giant sequins lay scattered on their frothy crests. There were a few white clouds in the sky. One group looked like a fluffy *T.Rex* dinosaur chasing smaller tennis ball clouds.

I was humming, that blasted *Kalinka* again. Misty Joy was trying to escape the sound by sticking her head out the window. I had always had a good ear for music but when the notes reached my vocal cords, something terribly strange happened to them. They always came out about a quarter of a tone off. Tara, the Rottweiler we had had before we got Misty, used to howl when I started to sing.

We turned south out of our driveway and headed for the rink. Most of the morning commute traffic was gone and we enjoyed the drive. My earlier grumpiness departed in the pleasure of the morning and the glory of the day. Not even the threat of another argument with Juliet Taggert was going to disturb me.

I pulled into the parking lot only to have a problem finding a spot to park. There were cars and vans all over the place, the vans sprouting giant coat hangers and saucer-like appendages. Etienne was standing, besieged, on the top step before the front door. Paul was trying to hide behind him to avoid questions by the media, to no avail.

"Paul, did you and Tami split up? Are you looking for a new partner?" shouted one diminutive female.

"Did you argue over coming here to Miki and Sheli?" asked another reporter, trying to shove a microphone at the bewildered skater, "Why did you two decide to leave Vaughan Pike? After all, he had coached you both since you started skating pairs."

These questions were very pointed and showed either some fast research or reporters who were seriously involved in the skating world. I wondered how the news of the disappearance had gotten out.

Paul Light and Tami Tompson were touted to be the United States' best hope for an Olympic medal in pairs next year in 1994. They had won Nationals this year in a surprising upset, and then gone on to place fifth at the World championships a month later. And, as the reporter had said, the very famous Vaughan Pike had been their coach since they had started skating pairs seriously.

Like most pair teams, they had started out as singles skaters. They both desperately wanted to compete at the international level. As individuals they probably wouldn't have made it. Several years ago, Vaughan had suggested they try skating together. Both skaters are tall, exceptionally so in a sport that seems to attract mighty mites. Paul, at six feet four inches, always looked as if he were going to run out of ice, especially during competition warm-ups while on the ice with his shorter contemporaries. Tami is five feet seven inches, again, much taller than her rivals.

Together, they made an imposing team. They were fearless on the ice. Their repertoire included two side by side triple jumps in their long program, when only the very best were trying one. Their throw jumps were spectacular, with Tami landing seemingly a mile from where she took off. Their musical interpretation was superb, skating with great feeling without overdramatizing the number.

They had left Vaughan for private reasons. Not something either of them wanted made public. Nor, I was certain, did Pike. He had been a coach of champions for many years with young hopefuls trekking to his rink in droves. He had been one of the big names we were hoping would join us at *N'ice Skates*. However, over the past year he had become increasingly erratic in his behavior, not showing up for lessons, insulting not only his skaters but others with equal fervor. Most incredibly, international judges were not immune to his tongue lashings, either.

The atmosphere in his arena had changed. It was no longer conducive to serious training. The skaters never knew if Vaughan would be in a good mood or ranting at all and sundry in his path. He had also decided that he could teach the overhead lifts better if he did the lifts himself on the ice with no floor practice. This last insanity was what had finally driven Paul and Tami away. He had tried to get Tami to do a star lift with a complicated exit with him and she refused. He was, after all, shorter than she was and close to 60 years old. The resulting confrontation left the pair in tears with no choice but to go somewhere else to train.

They had chosen *N'ice Skates*. We had been thrilled. Miki and Sheli would be good for them, we knew. Now, this circus!

Etienne was trying to get the attention of the reporters. Unfortunately he was speaking French again. Paul took advantage of my arrival to scuttle through the door as Misty Joy and I pushed our way through the crowd and entered the arena. That's one nice thing about having a big dog that many people take to be a white German Shepherd. They give her plenty of space.

"Have you talked with Mr. and Mrs. Tompson this morning, Paul? Are they coming out here?"

"They called me at home. There was a tape of Tami! It was delivered to the morning television news. CNN!"

"Who has her? Does anyone know? What do they want for her? What was it?"

"It was a video tape with Tami reading a short statement. She kept looking off to the side. Someone must have been with her. She said there would be another tape in two days with the kidnapper's demands. The FBI called me before I left the house. The guys from the San Francisco office are on their way down."

"Has anyone tried to get in touch with Vaughan Pike?"

"One of the reporters said that there was no answer at the rink or at his house."

Etienne scooted into the rink, pulling the door closed as fast as possible. "What do we do now?" he asked of no one in particular.

Gillian was already in the office answering the phone. It seemed a particularly futile occupation, especially since she couldn't keep up with all the calls. She spotted 'Tienne through the window and wagged her arm violently.

"I think Gillian wants you," I said. "She seems really agitated."

He lifted his arms, palms out, and gave a very Gallic shrug and started in to the office. Deputy Sean Mather stormed into the rink just at that moment. "Why didn't you tell us about Ms. Tompson's disappearance yesterday? Don't you understand that every minute is important in a kidnapping? I always thought skaters were screwballs. Now I know it! And we find out about it from the damn FBI. Now we'll have them in our hair."

"We didn't know she had been kidnapped. She left a note on her door frame. Told me she'd be in touch with me. We just thought her parents had needed her at home and we couldn't reach them last night. This morning was too late," Paul answered grumpily.

All hell was breaking loose outside. Naturally, Mrs. Taggert arrived with Brandi in tow and plowed her way through the mob outside. Other skaters were on the ice. Several youngsters went dutifully around in circles on the far rink. There was even one young girl working on eighth test figures, the highest figure test possible. Not many kids went that high anymore even though those figures were the fun ones, complicated, exacting and exhilarating.

Brandi was supposed to be over there working on her second test. It wasn't like them to be late. Just then they bustled in.

"Get your figure skates on, Brandi," snapped her mother. "We're already behind schedule. I have to talk to Berrien and Mr. Lepardieux."

Deputy Mather had other ideas and hustled Etienne into the office where Gillian was still wearing out her fingers punching phone buttons. I started in myself but found the door closed firmly and none-to-gently in my face, leaving me to face Juliet on my own. Since the only certain way to avoid another session with the mother was to give the daughter a figure lesson I excused myself quickly.

"Just let me go get my skates on, Brandi and we'll work on that left back serpentine. I think I've figured a way to correct your little problem." With that I dashed to the coaches' locker room and settled down in a big, comfortable chair to catch my breath. Misty, horse-sized as she was, climbed up beside me and laid her head—and shoulders—on my lap.

The pros' locker room was another luxury that we owners had given ourselves. We all spent many hours at the rink, some of it unpredictable down-time when students cancelled lessons or were out due to injury or school events. In most arenas the coaches had one small bench, minuscule lockers, no heat and the public rest rooms down the hall.

The architects had designed a cozy room with comfortable furniture, regulation lockers hidden behind real wood doors, a gas fireplace, tables, lamps and best of all, his and her bathrooms, complete with showers.

A few minutes of relaxation gave me some energy. Enough at least to get my skates on and go out and cope with Brandi's problem figure. I suspected that there would be considerably more serious problems that would rear their ugly heads in the very near future.

Just as I was getting ready to go out, Miki and Sheli came in. "Berrien, what are we going to do? This is terrible!" cried Sheli.

"Right at the moment, there's not much we can do. We'll just have to wait for Mr. and Mrs. Tompson and for the FBI. Has your mother arrived or are you going to fly up to get her?" I asked, well aware of the uproar the authoritarian Mrs. Andrade would cause when she descended on us. "If you're sure the body is your Uncle Tomaso, it might be better to head her off at the pass, if you can."

"She called right after the tape was run on the TV this morning. She said she was leaving right away. Not just to identify Uncle Tomaso, though. She is going to try to butt into this other business, too. She said she was sure Tomaso's death was part of a plot to harm our reputations and that Tami's problem—that's what she called it, a problem—was also part and parcel of the whole scheme!"

"Sounds like something she'd say. Is she going to stay at your place or are you getting her a room in Half Moon Bay?"

Miki and Sheli had bought a charming but rundown Victorian house in Portugal and were still in the process of renovating it. The kitchen had been finished, along with its one bath and the addition of a second one but the bedrooms were still pretty primitive. Last summer they had had a new roof put on and the exterior painted but Mrs. Andrade would not enjoy the upheaval so I thought they would be safe.

Miki surprised me. "Oh, she's announced that she'll stay with us. To protect us! It should be a whole lot of laughs."

With that cheerful thought the two dark-haired skaters wandered out into the arena again, looking miserable. It was unusual to see them so down. During their days in competition, Sheli's giggle and Miki's wonderful, wholehearted laugh had been heard in ice arenas around the world, in hotels and walking down the streets of host cities. On the ice they had been fearless. Like zygotic twins, rather than the fraternal twins they were, Sheli was left-handed and Miki used his right hand. Sheli spun and jumped to the right and Miki to the left. One of their most spectacular, although not technically difficult, moves was a pair of split jumps where their backs almost touched. It scared me witless every time I saw it.

I stepped outside the room cautiously, looking for Mrs. Taggert. She wasn't visible so I scuttled for the ice and went to Brandi's patch. While we were working on her problem school figure, I saw three people come in the front door. Three shades of grey suits, one daringly pinstriped, three variations of red paisley power ties, the lady had a paisley scarf, and three immaculately coiffed heads gave me their identification right away. As well as telling everyone in the arena who wasn't already aware of it that we had a serious problem.

Of course, with the media hoop-la outside, growing hourly, everyone on the Coast was going to know something odd was going on. It looked like we were running out of parking spaces. I hoped Etienne would get a word in with Mather about making them move away, at least some of them. We had a school group coming in for an afternoon public session and we'd need those parking spaces.

David was down the ice with the young lady who was working on her eighth test figures. We caught each other's eye and shrugged. The problem was out of our hands.

The three FBI agents went into the office where Etienne was still talking to Deputy Mather. Paul was pacing the floor. I finished with Brandi's lesson and went over to check on another student who was having some problems with a nasty figure called "threes to the center."

The figure must have been invented by the Marquis de Sade. On the first test, it largely determines if a skater is going to stick it out in school figures. The skater has to be a contortionist to do it according to the skater's bible, the USFSA Rulebook. Tommy wasn't—a contortionist, that is—and was consequently doing it wrong. The only thing useful about the position necessary for performing this particular maneuver is that it is good exercise for the waistline. We spent a few minutes on it and Tommy finally came up with a reasonable approximation of the correct tracing on the ice.

The rest of the morning passed uneventfully. Miki and Sheli were giving freestyle lessons to beginning pairs teams and David was back working with his dance team on the "Blues" so that they could, hopefully, pass their pre-Gold dance test the following week.

Marguerita wasn't expected until later in the day. Her mother and father insisted that she attend her regular school. Brandi, on the other hand, was being privately tutored as were several other young skaters. We had even included a small classroom in the plans for the complex and it was here that the teachers and skaters gathered for lessons.

Brandi's tutor had called to say she was ill so we had time to work on the show program that we had designed the day before. I told her to change her skates and get warmed up. "Don't forget the stretches before you get on the ice."

Gillian had her head poked out the office door. "Berrien, Etienne wants you in here, now."

"Okay. Let me get my skates off and I'll be right there," I replied, grateful for an excuse to get away before Juilet Taggert pounced. I knew that when she realized the music was the same as yesterday's there was going to be an explosion.

I went through the office and into 'Tienne's private lair. Big as it was, it seemed crowded with Deputy Mather, the three FBI agents and Etienne sitting around on all the available chairs. Mather did the honors, introducing me to the governmental contingent, Mr. Watson, the one with the pin-stripe suit, Ms. Mosovich with her paisley scarf, and Mr. Stanley.

"How do you do?" asked the three, almost in unison. Not waiting for any answer Mr. Watson continued, "We understand you found a body here yesterday. Why?"

Why? What a stupid question. And how was I supposed to answer it?

"Well, actually, I didn't find the body. Misty did." Deputy Mather's eyes rolled and he had trouble keeping from laughing, having been caught the same way the day before.

Mr. Watson turned to the deputy, "Why did you tell us this lady found the corpse? Who is Misty? We need her in here right now. You may go, Ms. Gamble."

I turned to leave, then asked, "Do you want me to get Misty for you?"

"Of course," snapped Stanley, "I would think that would be obvious. Is she here in the building?"

"Yes, I'll bring her to you."

"You don't have to accompany her. Just send her in."

The big, white dog was sleeping peacefully, curled up in the chair where I had left her over an hour earlier. She woke up as I came in and stretched luxuriously. "Come on, Misty. Your presence is requested by the FBI."

We walked back to the office and Gillian opened 'Tienne's door. Misty adored our manager and was accustomed to spending a lot of time with him. What with one thing and another she hadn't seen much of him the past two days. She bounded in and jumped in his lap.

Deputy Mather gravely introduced her to Agents Watson, Stanley and Mosovich. The dog, always friendly, wagged her tail toward the non-plussed law officers.

Gillian said she could hear the roar of anger in her office. Since I had stayed outside in the arena I missed it. Fortunately, Gillian called me to come in. I was glad to go. Mrs. Taggert was bearing down on me at a speed made dangerous by the high-heeled, backless sandals she was wearing.

Mr. Watson was upset. Actually, insulted is a better word. "Ms. Gamble, is this your idea of a joke? If so, you have a very twisted sense of humor!"

"Sorry, Mr. Watson. I was just following your orders. Misty did find the body out on the ice. But what's that got to do with Tami's kidnapping? Surely someone who would kill an old tramp didn't abduct a champion figure skater."

"We don't know if they're connected, but we have to look at everything unusual that's happened in the last few days."

Etienne explained how Misty came to be on the ice and the rest of yesterday's sequence of events. The federal agents then decided that neither my services nor those of my dog were required any longer and dismissed us.

"But be sure to remain available," reminded Ms. Mosovich sternly.

We swept out the door, Misty with her tail wagging gaily managed to deposit great clumps of long white fur on the three fine grey wool suits to remember her by.

Outside, Juliet Taggert was still waiting, far from patiently. "What is going on? The media certainly aren't here over that bum you found yesterday."

She had to be the only person on the Coast who hadn't either seen the story on CNN in the morning or heard about it here at the rink. Of course, Juliet wasn't anyone's favorite person. Her husband was very rich and they lived in the biggest house in the area, a fact she was sure to mention to anyone new. Her clothes were almost as much of a disaster as Brandi's skating dresses. She apparently had nothing informal to wear and always looked as though she was heading for a cocktail party. I doubted that any of the parents scattered around the complex ever had much to say to her.

"No, Juliet. It's not about that. Tami Tompson has apparently been kidnapped. Paul says that she was on television this morning reading the demand for her safety."

"How awful! We must get a bodyguard for Brandi. How much do the kidnappers want for her? Why did they take her? Everyone knows that her family has no money. She even works as a waitress over at the Anchor Bar!"

"Whoever has her isn't demanding money. They aren't demanding anything, yet. There's supposed to be another tape sent to us in two days."

"What a strange ransom. Oh, well. Enough of that. I want to be sure that you are going to make Brandi's solo longer. And isn't that number being rehearsed tonight? I'd better call James and make sure we have a guard for Brandi before then."

"Juliet, to answer your questions in order, Brandi's solo is in a production number. I'm not going to recut the whole thing to make her part longer. Now, if you don't want her to skate it, I'll give it to someone else. And rehearsal starts at five for two hours. I'll see you then."

Just then Gillian stuck her head out the door again. "Miki, Sheli! The FBI wants to talk to you," she bellowed at the two who were about two hundred feet away.

Miki shouted just as loudly, "We'll be there in a minute."

With perfect timing, the main door opened to allow their mother to stride in purposefully. "You'll be right where?" she screeched.

Mrs. Andrade didn't walk anyplace. She marched, stalked or paraded. She was, as always, enveloped in a miasma of *Joy* perfume. It had always been one of my favorites until I met her. A little bit of it goes a long way. This lady didn't believe that and went through several large bottles of the stuff every year. I switched to a rose fragrance.

With a toss of her bleached blond hair, Juliet left to collect Brandi and presumably corral a bodyguard or two. Just what the poor child needed to complete her isolation from the other skaters.

Sheli, Miki and their mother went in to talk to the federal agents. I was sure that Rosa Andrade was going to be thrown out shortly.

I was right. She came out followed by Deputy Mather who towered over the tiny woman. It was an oddly matched pair. Her worn, faded blue jeans, sprayed on her rigidly kept body, were almost the same color as the deputy's silver grey uniform trousers. The powder blue ski jacket she wore matched the blue shirt that Mather had on.

As usual she was talking. "I should be in there. Those are my children!"

"Yes, but they're adults, aren't they?" he asked.

"They need my advice. I've always protected them."

"Don't worry, Mrs. Andrade. The agents just need a time frame. Miki and Sheli aren't suspected of anything."

Chapter 7

Misty and I got into the car. I had decided to go get some lunch for everyone involved in the question and answer session. We drove along the highway just above the water. The ocean was having its usual calming effect on me. Who needed psychiatrists when you lived in close proximity to the rhythm of crashing waves.

I looked around the countryside. Old barns with most all of the paint gone except for some faint indications of advertising, the kind seen in any rural area of the country, were all over the place. Rusting farm equipment of various, and to me mysterious, uses sat forlorn and lonely. Acres of land, used for generations to grow large crops of vegetables and flowers for the population of San Francisco and San Mateo counties, lay idle, only unidentifiable weeds growing listlessly along the rail fencing.

Every few hundred yards were closed-up roadside stands, used to sell vegetables, fruits and flowers to the tourists who drive along the coast every Spring and Summer. Pumpkins are a big item in October. In fact, Half Moon Bay has a big Pumpkin Festival every year and the whole

Coast comes to life then. There were painted signs above the shuttered windows promising fresh strawberries, carrots and peas. The sign that always amused me guaranteed freshly picked bananas!

The town of Portugal looked more crowded than usual. Then I realized that reporters, both print and television were crowding the sidewalks, microphones or pencils at the ready, trying to interview the townspeople. Most of them were shaking their heads and walking away.

One lady who had been adamantly opposed to the complex spotted me and came over as I got out of the car.

"Oh, Berrien. This is just awful. I hope that nice young lady will be okay. If there's anything we can do to help, please call. We're all behind you."

Almost speechless from this evidence of support, I managed to stutter, "Thank you. We hope she'll be all right, too. Sorry about all this circus."

"Oh, don't let that worry you. We protect our own and you've done everything you said you would. The town is better off with you all here. The rink is part of the town now."

Considerably lighter in heart after that short conversation, I went into the general store. I had lived most summers of my youth in a small town on the Eastern Shore of Maryland. This store was three thousand miles away but looked and smelled just like the Cheffins General Store had many years ago. The pickle barrel stood open, full of delectable briny cucumbers. Several shelves held bolts of Dan River cotton fabrics, the patterns unchanging over the years. Hardware items for the rusting equipment on the deserted farms were carefully placed in their respective bins. There was even an old Coke dispenser with real bottles of Coke, chilled and waiting.

Something new had been added in the past two years. At the back was a modern delicatessen. Meats, vegetables and salads were on display here. An old-fashioned slate board held the daily special choices. Today the sandwich was their special crab salad sandwich. Made with fresh crab, homemade mayonnaise, crisp celery and pickled garlic from Gilroy, it was a feast on a bun, or in my case a Dutch Crunch roll.

Not sure of Deputy Mather's preferences, nor that of the FBI people, I ordered several crab sandwiches plus three with roast beef—with everything—and three turkey with only tomato and lettuce, to go, of course. And I got an extra cup of crab salad for Misty Joy, who, being part Japanese, loves fish of any kind, but is especially fond of crab. I took a whole carrot cake, too, for dessert.

The pink and black nose was sticking out the car window as I struggled back through the throngs of reporters and their ancillary appendages.

"Berrien, what's being done about Tami?" shouted one young man whose face was familiar to me. He was a reporter for a San Francisco station.

Above his voice, partially overriding the question was another, more imperious baritone. "Come over and give us an interview. We'll put it on the six o'clock national news."

Not a request, mind you, but a demand.

Shaking my head, I got to the car and opened the door just as a short, stocky man about sixty years old grabbed my arm. "See! You bunch of hicks can't keep a skater safe! When Tami's found I'll get the team back at my rink."

"Let go of me, you fool. The cameras are catching every bit of this, Vaughan. Come out to the rink if you want to but let go of me now!" He raised the hand that wasn't gripping my right elbow as if to strike me. A white streak of fur flashed out the partially opened door to grab Vaughan's wrist in a none-too-gentle mouth. No bark, no growl, just swift movement.

"I'll sue you for this. It was an unprovoked attack by that vicious animal on me!" he shouted.

"Misty, let go. It's okay. Get in the car." She let go of the pro's wrist and jumped back onto the seat. I loaded the sack of food in and we left Pike standing there still screaming threats with the cameras rolling and the microphones waving almost in unison, just like a precision drill team kick line.

I drove about a mile towards the arena and then began to shake. I pulled over into a little side road that faced the ocean and just sat there. Misty Joy nuzzled my neck, kissed my face and wiggled her considerable bulk onto my lap.

There had been stories recently about Pike and his rages but the skating world had managed to keep it quiet for the most part. After today's all-too-public eruption it was certainly no longer his private problem.

The shaking stopped as I scratched the dog's ears. "Good girl, Misty Joy. Thank you." She wasn't at all sure that she had done the right thing. Never before in her life had she attacked anyone or anything. Next to her "skating" she best loved to play with other dogs and had even made friends with an aloof Siamese cat named Isis who reigned at Miki and Sheli's place.

Calmer, although still upset over the confrontation, I pulled back onto the highway to deliver lunch. The parking lot was more crowded than ever but I managed to park in the last space available.

The federal contingent of law officers was still in Etienne's office, talking to Mather now. I poked my head into Gillian's room. "Gillian, tell the officers and Etienne that I have lunch for anyone interested. Have them come down to the pros' room."

Since it was now around two o'clock, everyone must have been hungry. Misty and I were followed closely by Mather, Etienne and the three FBI agents. David waved to me from the ice. "Come get some lunch, David."

"Sounds good. I'll be there in five minutes."

I put the sack of sandwiches and cake on the table *cum* desk that we had supplied ourselves with. Miki and Sheli, considerably younger that most of the pros, had wanted to get a computer, too. We had vetoed the idea. Most of us were severely "technologically challenged" and didn't want any reminders of our incipient helplessness in the modern world.

Paper plates and plastic forks were kept in an unused locker. I got them out and set out the impromptu buffet, grabbing my crab sandwich and Misty's cup of crab first. She had earned her treat.

Everyone took a sandwich and got a cup of coffee from the ever-warming pot on a back table and sat down around the big table.

It was time to drop my bombshell. Turning to Mr. Watson I asked, "Do you know where Vaughan Pike is now?"

"Who's Vaughan Pike?"

"Paul and Tami's former coach."

"Should we be worried about where he is? And if so, why?"

Sheli said, "Well, he was definitely not happy over losing them. He's made some nasty calls to Miki and me. Called us thieves and a few less complimentary names."

"He also just called us hicks on national television," I remarked.

Watson swung to look at me. "What do you mean? When did you see this? Where is he?"

"He was busy attacking me both verbally and physically in town about a half an hour ago. The media were going bananas over it. He was going to hit me but Misty bit his wrist."

"Whoa, whoa. Back up and start from the beginning," suggested Ms. Mosovich.

I described the fracas in town and even displayed the bruise Pike's strong hand had caused on my elbow. In case he did sue me for Misty's bite I figured it wouldn't hurt to have federal agents see the evidence on me.

Miki had been sitting quietly, enjoying the overfull roast beef sandwich. Suddenly he said, "I wonder what the hell he's doing here? It's a long flight out here from his rink. He can't be so hung up on Tami and Paul that he got out here to give any kind of help. He's still got a whole rink full of skaters to coach."

Mr. Stanley regarded him questioningly, then got up. "I think I'll take a drive into town. Where did you say you saw this Mr....mm Pike, Ms. Gamble?"

"By the general store. He was outside, around where one of the networks has a big setup."

Stanley walked out the door just as Rosa Andrade pushed her way in. "There you are," she warbled as she ruffled Miki's hair with one hand and grabbed the last turkey sandwich with the other. "I'm so hungry I could eat a cow. Didn't even stop for breakfast this morning. As soon as I saw that TV news thing I just hopped in the car and drove here fast as I could. The traffic was terrible. A big truck overturned, one of those logging trucks. Took an hour to clear it. We're going to have to get a four lane road up there."

She finally stopped long enough to take a gigantic bite of the sandwich. The rest of us took the opportunity to leave the room, cowards that we were, leaving poor Miki and Sheli with their mother.

The school group was whooping it up, flopping about on the ice and screaming as only fifty first graders can. They were having a ball. David, Etienne and I rushed onto the ice to get some organization into the group. Children always seem to leave their shoe laces undone unless there is Velcro someplace. They had done the same with their skates. The laces were slipping under their blades and bringing them to a rapid halt. Every time a kid would try to get up he would be tripped again by the loose laces.

We got them all tied into their skates and retreated to the office.

What a day, and we still had two hours of rehearsal to go with one hundred and twenty five kids to keep focused. I went to the music room to recheck the music and get the notes on the movements that had already been finished. I hoped we could finish the choreography of this number so we could get started on the Russian number at the next meeting.

At the appointed hour, Etienne and I got out on the freshly-made ice. The cast of the Oriental number was swirling around, showing off for each other and watching 'Tienne and me closely. They were, in effect, hoping to snag some solo time themselves.

Mrs. Taggert swept back into the rink with Brandi in tow. Juliet was clad in lime green sand-washed silk slacks and a matching blouse with a precariously low neckline. Her backless sandals had even higher heels than the ones she had worn earlier in the day. Brandi had on a matching lime green skating dress dripping with large aurora crystal beads. I hoped she didn't fall on them.

They were trailed by a tall, thin man dressed in a pair of jeans, cowboy boots with real leather heels, some sort of shirt with a white collar which just showed above the heavy Aran sweater. His eyes looked everywhere. Juliet had done it. Gotten a bodyguard.

Finally, everyone was on the ice. Miki and Sheli had come out to help, too. Deputy Mather had finally taken their mother over to the coroner's office to see if the body we had found yesterday was indeed her brother, Tomaso.

I started the music. The introduction flooded the arena with the lovely strains from *The Yellow River Concerto*.

We did a run through of the first half of the number. Wonder of wonders, almost everyone got into the correct positions and stopped where we had ended at the last practice. Then the work really started as we led each group of children through the steps I had designed. The groups were divided roughly by age and abilities so the moves were set up by degree of difficulty.

"Brandi, that was terrific!" I called to her after she had skated her solo part. "You skated better than I have ever seen you skate."

Her plain face fairly bloomed at the compliment. Her mother, sitting in the stands with the bodyguard, opened her mouth and was apparently talking but I couldn't hear her over the music. Thank goodness.

The March of the Siamese Children began and the little children, three to five years old did their part of the number. The varying degrees of mobility of the various children caused the usual stops and starts as the skaters got into their circle. Several fell but that was to be expected. On show nights it would add to what I called the "adorable factor." Then came the finale with the entire group on the ice, moving to more music from *The Yellow River Concerto*. I could just see it with the costumes I had planned, yellows, reds and greens, with black trimmings.

We ran through it again. Then it was time for the Junior Drill Team to take the ice. Their number was skated to a disco version of *Over the Rainbow*. The costumes would be all sequins in rainbow colors. Brandi and Marguerita were both in this number and would have enough glitter to satisfy even Juliet.

Etienne was exhausted with worry and was being somewhat less than his most charming self. Parents were hanging over the railings. We had had a few problems with our manager and the parents. He was always great with the kids but didn't hesitate to use impolite words in both French and English to the proud mothers and dads when he felt they were butting in. After the past two days, Miki, Sheli, David and I were trying to run interference so that the parental group and the choreographer didn't run afoul of one another. We didn't need any bad feelings.

The girls finally did a satisfactory run through of the program, thank goodness. Etienne had been getting very edgy and was about ready to have one of his trademark fits. Everyone got off the ice just as the arena opened for public session.

Hoards of people trooped through the door. Visitors who had never been to the rink. Many weren't even going to skate—if, in fact, they knew how. They just wanted to be at the scene of a crime, or at least as close to it as they could get. Those few who had brought their own skates or rented some, quickly got them on and skated out to the hockey circle where Uncle Tomaso had been found.

Feeling weary, I decided to get home quickly and headed for the pros' room. So did the others. We slid inside.

"With all those gawkers out there how do you plan to get Misty out of here in one piece? I bet she was featured on the news tonight!" Sheli said.

"What an encouraging thought! Thanks a lot, Sheli."

"She's right," agreed Miki.

"I know, but I sure don't want her mobbed. She did what she thought was right and didn't really hurt Pike. At least I don't think so. We should have had a door to the outside put in this room."

"Well, we didn't. If we all go out together and keep the dog in between us, we ought to make it," David suggested.

We adopted that plan as the only one available and walked out of the room in a clump, surrounding Misty Joy. It would have worked, too, if it hadn't been for that great plume of a tail. It stuck out behind David, wagging frenetically, attracting more attention than we all would have if we had walked her out openly.

"Hey, mister. I seen that dog on television," a young boy said, ungrammatically, to David. "Does it bite lots of people or just old men?"

I was sure Pike would have loved to have heard that! Actually I wasn't too pleased either and David was always sensitive about getting older. Miki and Sheli laughed—well, they could, they were still on the early side of thirty.

The comment did, however, allow us to hurry through the throngs of lookers and skaters.

Miki and Sheli split up, he to the jeep and Sheli to drive their mother's car home. The deputy was to deliver her in person, later on.

Chapter 8

The phone was ringing as we walked in the door. The machine picked it up and I turned the volume up to hear who was calling.

"Berrien, where are you? I've just seen the news from home! How did you manage to get involved in a kidnapping? I've only been gone three days! It was a shock to see Misty biting someone. Couldn't you have called me?"

"Hi, darlin'," I answered. "I'm glad I caught your call. We just this minute walked in. How're your meetings going? Are you still ahead of schedule?"

"Don't soft soap me. What have you gotten yourself into now? Are you all right?"

"Okay, you've heard about the kidnapping right?"

"Yes." It was clipped, short. Philip trying to keep his temper.

I took a deep breath and asked, "Did they say anything about the dead body we found yesterday morning?"

"Dead body! What dead body? Whose dead body? Who found this dead body?"

"Sheli thinks it's their Uncle Tomaso. Mrs. Andrade came down today so we should know definitely soon. He was just lying out on the ice, dead. I went to the rink early to do the Russian production music before everyone got there. Misty did one of her numbers on the ice and slid right into him. We've had the cops around so much I think we're going to have to give them free lessons. You should have seen the poor coroner guy when he saw where the body was. Right in the middle of the ice!"

"Are you sure you're okay?"

"Of course I am. Nothing's happened to me. Well, Vaughan Pike saw me in town today. He wasn't very nice and bruised my elbow. That's why Misty bit him, he looked like he was going to hit me."

"Now, tell me about Tami. How did all of this happen and when?"

Engineers! Everything in life should be reduced to formulas and numbers. No questions to be left unanswered.

"We don't know when she was kidnapped or how. Her Mom and Dad are supposed to be out here but I haven't seen them today. Maybe the FBI knows where they are. Poor Paul. He's a basket case."

"The FBI! Are they working on it too?"

"Of course. We're talking kidnapping. Of a United States champion, no less, Philip. They were crawling—no, they wouldn't do anything so undignified—they were at the rink all day today. From the San Francisco office, I think."

"Should I come home now?"

"Oh, for heaven's sake, why? You're not finished with your conferences, are you? We have everything at the rink under control."

"It certainly doesn't sound like it!" snapped my exasperated husband from seventy-five hundred miles away.

I heard a scratching at the kitchen door. "Honey, hold on. Let me get the portable phone. Misty wants to go out and we both need dinner. The rehearsal was exhausting. And Juliet Taggert has now gotten a bodyguard for Brandi. I think her next project is a therapist to help the poor kid deal with all the trauma."

Philip snorted. "If you ask me, if Brandi has problems with trauma it probably started at birth given that woman for a mother!"

A sharp bark was obviously heard half way around the world. "Go let the mutt out. I'll wait while you get the other phone. And speaking of phones, when I get home, we're getting you a cell phone to carry around. I'm tired of talking to that damn machine!"

Just what I needed. Something else to cart around and remember to get batteries for. My car already served as home port to two portable music players, one tape and one CD, a portable radio, a large flashlight and a complete video taping system, all of which ran on different size batteries. The next thing Philip was going to suggest was a lap-top computer to hook into the phone with Internet and e-mail access, whatever that is when it's at home.

I let Misty out and picked up the portable phone. "You know, my love, these phones aren't exactly the kind of things you want to have private discussions on. I understand they're easy to listen in on," I warned as I wandered around the kitchen, trying to decide on something for dinner.

"I still want to hear the whole story. Does old Uncle Tomaso have anything to do with Tami's disappearance?"

"How would I know? Until Sheli and Miki went to see the body, we just thought it was some bum…and we didn't know Tami was gone either until that TV program this morning. That's all any of us know. We have media types coming out of the woodwork! They were even taping the Zambonis today while the ice was being made. As if they were somehow important! Can't you just see the eleven o'clock news, soft baritone voice over the awful racket they make. 'Now we take you to the arena on the California coast where there have been a number of mysterious happenings over the past several days'…fade to a shot of the

N'ice Skates sign? Oops, sorry, I've been trying to work out the lighting and script for the show. Got carried away."

"Berrien, you're babbling. You really are upset, aren't you?"

"Of course. It's all such a mess. At this point I'm wondering what's going to happen tomorrow. Look, honey, this call is costing someone a fortune. We'd better cut it short. Do you know when you'll be back?"

"The end of this week, Monday, probably."

"Your Monday or the one here?"

"Yours. Tuesday here in Sydney."

"Maybe when all this is cleared up we can go someplace for a few days. Kauai sounds like a wonderful idea."

"Okay, darling. We'll do that. I'll call you before I leave here. Tell you what flight to meet. G'dey."

"'Night, Philip. I love you."

It was good to talk to my husband. He always had a way of getting me to think rather than react emotionally. Now I could settle down, get some dinner and get a good night's sleep.

Misty came in, looking for her dinner. I poured out the venison kibble that is her staple and added half a can of its matching moist food. Boy, did that disappear fast.

I really didn't feel like cooking and thought how simple it would be if we ate like our pets. The refrigerator had nothing exciting in it. An omelet was going to have to do. There was some salsa hidden behind the Kona coffee that would be good over it.

Kitchen duty done and dinners eaten, we headed for the master bedroom. Misty Joy's toenails clicked on the hand-made tile floor of the long hallway, as we walked to the extreme far end of the house. Our way was lighted by the moon shining through the house-long skylight.

I had forgotten to make the bed in the morning and the room looked rumpled and forlorn. I straightened the comforter and went in to run a bath in the large tub and turned the jets on. My back was still hurting and a good long soak was definitely in order. The drapes in both the bedroom and the bathroom were open. We rarely closed them as our nearest neighbors on that side of the house were in Hawaii.

The waves, only a hundred yards away, were crashing against the rocks as I lay in the tub. The gentle hum of the Jacuzzi motor was lulling me to sleep. I sat up abruptly, sputtering. The past two days had been exhausting and I really needed some sleep rather than drowning myself in the tub.

Despite its still messy state, the bed looked inviting. I fell into it and invited Misty to join me. She really preferred her own big basket but sometimes when she sensed my need she would condescend to share the big, king-sized thing with me. She jumped up and curled herself in a big ball on my pillow.

The moon, for once not hidden by fog, was shining on the ocean, I could see the waves from the bed, streaked with white froth and moonshine. The sight and sound of the peaceful scene lulled me to sleep.

A sharp jab in the region of my ribs, along with a very nasty, loud growl pulled me out of a dream where I was loaded down with roses, taking bow after bow at the closing night of the show. Misty had jumped off the bed, using my rib cage as the launching pad, and was standing by the sliding door to the deck. The moon was still visible and I could see a moving shadow outside. It was heading on down the deck towards the other end of the house.

Misty was barking. Akitas don't bark very often. When they do, it is serious business. Misty Joy had inherited this trait from her Akita father. She very rarely made any noise. To hear her now was frightening. What it was doing to the would-be intruder was anyone's guess. It didn't seem to be discouraging him—or her—however. I could hear the doors being tested along the whole length of the house.

I fumbled for the phone and dialled 911. With a great deal of reluctance. More confrontation with the Sheriff's office was not number one on my want list. While identifying myself and giving the information the dispatcher was asking for, I rooted in the drawers of the desk that does double duty as my bed table.

Like many people who are alone a lot at night I had a gun. It was usually kept loaded and I was trying to remember if I had reloaded it after its last cleaning while I finished the emergency call. The very first rule of gun use, as my father taught me, was *never* aim an unloaded weapon at someone. My hand found the thirty-eight under several tons of paper and I pulled it out. Checked it. It wasn't loaded. I felt around in the drawer looking for the ammunition.

The dog was barking even more violently. I went over to the door out to the deck and flicked all the lights on outside. The whole area was brilliant with man-made stars.

I could see the figure stumble in the unexpected illumination and put hands up to its' eyes. It was impossible to tell if it was a man or a woman. All I could see were dark trousers and some kind of long, all-weather coat in universal light brown or beige. A baseball cap was pulled down low on the stranger's forehead. I guessed maybe five feet six or seven. The feet were blurry so the sneakers were probably black.

The sirens could be heard a long way off in the still of the early morning. The figure heard them, too. It stood still, startled again. Why, I couldn't figure out. Did he (or she) expect me to invite him (or her) in for a cozy chat? Then I heard pounding footsteps on the deck as the person flashed by the bedroom window. There was a cry as someone missed the steps and slid off the unprotected deck. That was followed by a string of words that wouldn't have been unfamiliar to a longshoreman. It was a man's voice. At least that's what it sounded like. I could hear more pounding on our gravel driveway, but now it was uneven, as though the intruder has hurt a leg or ankle. I hoped so.

Misty had been following the retreat room by room and was back in the bedroom, quiet now except for loud panting. She flopped on her bed and looked at me. Twice in one day she had been called upon to act in a manner totally foreign to her usual, easygoing self. I got down on the floor and patted her, reassuring her, and myself, that everything was all right.

The doorbell rang, startling both of us. I had forgotten about calling the police. We started to the front door, Misty so close to me I almost fell over her. I put on the front lights and saw a big, unfamiliar deputy standing outside. I opened the door, "Come in. Thanks for coming but he got scared off by your siren."

He stood on the doorstep, still. Slowly, he held his hands out to his sides. "Okay, ma'am. Everything is okay. Now, please put the gun down. You don't need it. Put the gun down."

What was he talking about? Then I realized that the thirty-eight was still clutched in my hand. Totally harmless, not only no bullets but the cylinder was hanging loose, the way I had left it while trying to remember where the bullets were hidden.

What a fetching picture I must have made, standing in the doorway, useless firearm in hand and dressed to kill in my night attire of an old Half Moon Bay Pumpkin Festival extra long tee shirt.

I put the gun down on the umbrella stand by the doorway and once again invited the deputy in. More relaxed now, he accepted the invitation and came inside. I waved toward the kitchen. "Go on into the family room. It's cold. I'd better get a robe on." With that I dashed to the bedroom to find an adult type of bathrobe.

More discretely attired, I made my way back down the hallway to the kitchen. The deputy was standing, unsure of what to do next as I flipped the lights on. "Have a seat. I'll get us some coffee. Would you like a bagel?"

"Maybe I'd better introduce myself. I'm Jonathan Martin," he said while showing me his badge and identification. "Can you tell me what has been happening. I just got a call about a prowler. First, may I have your name?"

"Oh, sure. Sorry. I'm Berrien Gamble."

"Where was this prowler?"

"Well, outside on the deck. Whoever it was went the whole length. Then he or she, I couldn't tell, must have fallen off when he came back to the bedroom area. We don't have any railing on it. A fence would have spoiled the view of the water. Anyhow, he got up and started running again, but it sounded like he was limping on the driveway."

"Have you had trouble like this with prowlers before now?"

"No, never. But after the last two days at work, I'm not surprised at anything."

"At work? Has there been trouble at your place of employment?"

"Some. There was the body on the ice and then Tami's kidnapping with the FBI all over the place today…no, I guess it must be yesterday," I said as I looked at the clock on the microwave. It was two o'clock in the morning.

"Oh, you must be the one with the skating dog!"

"Sure am. She's sitting right next to you."

"Okay, we'd better get back to this business. You say you couldn't identify this person? Male or female? Nothing?"

"No, the overcoat and dark trousers were about all. Oh, I could barely see the feet or hear any real steps, just the squeaking of the deck so the person must have had dark sneakers on. And a baseball-type cap pulled down low on the forehead."

"Did you hear a car or truck after he ran away?"

"No. Didn't you see anyone as you drove up the driveway? It sounded as if he was headed towards the road. There aren't any steps down to the water, at least not near here so he couldn't have gotten away there."

"Well, maybe he hid behind a tree or bush as I came up. I sure didn't see anyone, though. There was a small car parked on the side of the road about a quarter of a mile away. Didn't see anyone in it. Tell you what, let me go look around outside and I'll come back in. Leave all the lights on and lock the door after me. I'll knock when I get finished out there."

Deputy Martin went out the kitchen door which I then dutifully relocked and bolted. Misty once again followed the man outside, checking at every window in each room, but she wasn't barking now. She knew this one was supposed to be there. The deputy disappeared from her view as he went behind the bedroom wall but she soon found him as he carefully checked the bushes planted close to the front of the house. He was lost again as he went past the garage and finally materialized back at the kitchen door.

I opened it and he came back in.

"I didn't find anyone hiding out there but there sure was somebody out there tonight. I found a fresh bloodstain at the edge of the deck so you're right about the person getting hurt. Probably just a nosebleed or something. I've got it marked and we'll send one of the technicians out in the morning. And I'll check the car out down the road. At least get the license plate. Will you be okay here? Do you want to call someone to come stay with you?"

"Oh, no. I'll be all right. Whoever it was is probably long gone."

"Well, good night, then. Oh, and Ms. Gamble, may I make a suggestion?"

"Sure. What is it?"

"Either load that fool pistol or lose it!"

With that, I escorted him to the front door. Misty and I went back to bed, not believing that I would even blink an eyelid.

Chapter 9

I woke up to find my hand on the telephone by the bed. It was ringing and if telephones can be said to have personality problems, this one did. It sounded definitely peevish. I expected it to be ringing in Morse code, *pick me up, pick me up.*

I did. That was a mistake.

"Berrien, I 'ave decided to 'ave our pros meeting this morning. It is necessaire that we all talk about these 'orrible tings that are 'appening." Of course it was Etienne, not yet reduced to French but with a French accent reminiscent of Charles Boyer at his most Continental.

As I said, Etienne was renowned as an insomniac. I rolled over to look outside. The fog was back with a vengeance. It was pressing against the doors, trying to get in to the house. The clock said seven o'clock. We generally had our meetings on Fridays at the civilized hour of eleven.

"Etienne, what time are you planning this meeting for? I don't even want to try to drive in this fog. Have you looked out the windows yet this morning?"

"We meet at nine."

"Oh, come on. The pros that live over on the Peninsula aren't going to make it over the hill by then—even if they don't have something else planned for today."

"We must do something."

"Oh, all right, 'Tienne. I'll get there. See you later. And the meeting had better be in English!"

Etienne's "do something" sounded ominous. He had a reputation for crazy stunts going back to his days in *Ice Follies*. He had been known to jump from a second floor balcony into the motel swimming pool and once borrowed a line girl's costume so he could skate in the precision number. He got caught on that one because his wig fell off. The fine was a stiff one, particularly since he also paid the young lady's fine, too.

It wasn't beyond the realm of possibility for him to plan a raid to kidnap Tami back. That is, when she was found.

Realizing that I certainly wasn't going to get anymore sleep, I took a shower and got dressed. Skating coaches have a serious problem with clothes. We have to take the outside weather into consideration as well as the hours we are going to spend on the ice plus any other errands we need to attend to during the day. The obvious answer is layering the clothes, which works in colder weather. In the summertime over the years, I have gotten some very strange looks from neighbors who didn't know what my profession was as I got into my car loaded with sweaters and down parkas as the thermometer was reaching the 80's. Added to that, if there were going to be important skating people visiting, Etienne insisted that we all wear skating clothes. For the guys, that meant stretch trousers with elastic under the boots, a dress shirt and tie with a good-looking, patterned sweater. For the ladies, it meant a real skating dress, not a leotard and wrap-around skirt but the real thing, skin-tight, short and if we didn't keep moving, damn cold, too.

The fog made the clothing choice fairly easy. Wool slacks, a cotton, turtleneck top and a hand knit ski sweater. I keep a parka at the rink.

After a light breakfast, Misty and I set out for the arena. The fog had thinned slightly. I could see at least ten feet in front of me. No time for wool-gathering or worry about 'Tienne's screwy plans now. My eyes stayed glued to the road, glancing in the rear-view mirror frequently to make sure no idiot was racing up behind me.

Finally, I pulled into the arena parking lot. The media madness of yesterday was over, at least for the time being. The following day would probably bring a return visit if the proposed video tape showed up. Miki and Sheli were already there and David pulled in right behind me. His mouth was moving. I wondered if he was swearing at the disruption of his morning or singing in tune with the radio.

"Hi. What do you suppose the old boy is up to now?" I asked as we got out of our respective cars. "I sure hope he's not planning some hair-brained scheme. Wouldn't put it past him, though."

David laughed. He had known Etienne a lot longer than I had and so had a much better idea of the range of possibilities. "I wouldn't put anything past him. We are all going to have to sit on him, hard. I don't think the Sheriff's office or the FBI would want him interfering."

We walked into the office. Poor Gillian was still answering phone calls, although they seemed to be mostly from parents wanting assurances that their children weren't going to be kidnapped or murdered. None of the coaches who lived over on the San Francisco Bay side had arrived yet. It would be another half hour before they could make it.

"Hey, Miki," David called, "how did it go with your mother last night?"

"Just about like you would expect. Fights every time one of us opened our mouths. It was Uncle Tomaso, though. She was really upset over that. Not that he was dead, understand. But that he was a bum!"

"Did she learn what he died of?" Etienne joined in the conversation.

"Well, sorta. It's really strange. The coroner's not sure whether he died from a heart attack or strangling. There were signs that he was choked with his own scarf but he also had massive heart damage. They think that maybe the attack was brought on by the scarf pulled too tight around his neck. Fright, I guess. I guess we'll never know. But for whatever reason, they're calling it murder."

"Oh, wonderful," said 'Tienne caustically. "Not just a dead body, but a murdered dead body and a kidnapped skater. We finally get national publicity and look what it is. I knew I should have taken the offer to go to Sun Valley!"

"Did they say how he got on the ice? Have any theories, anything?" I asked.

Sheli said, "Well, they think he was dragged there. He wasn't killed out there. They think he was caught outside and dragged in. That's how one shoe got caught in the door. There were scrapes on the heel of the bare foot. Like he had been dragged."

"There's only that three and a half hour time span. You guys left at one thirty and I got here just after five."

"They think he might have been killed earlier than that and then pulled into the rink. At least that's what Mom heard them talking about. It's hard for them to tell because he was lying on the ice so long."

While we had been talking several other pros had arrived. Most of them taught classes and private lessons at other rinks in the Bay Area. They brought their students "over the hill" to practice on our ice because it was a regulation size rink and allowed their competitive skaters to get the feel of their programs on the proper size rink. This arrangement was unusual but we found that it worked well. Once we finished the dormitories and the rest of the complex we hoped the pros would move over to the Coast with their students. The weight trainer and the dance coach had also shown up. They usually came to the rink two or three times a week. Another plan that was only partly in place. We hoped to use them full time once everything was complete.

I could see out into the arena proper. Our Ladies Coffee Club was slowly gathering, talking as usual. This class was always fun. It had begun years ago at another rink where Etienne started teaching. The ladies were mainly skating mothers who sat endless hours on end watching their children practice. Many were quick to criticize their offspring for the least little problem. 'Tienne had gotten the idea to start a class just for them. It would give the mothers a chance to exercise and let them learn just how hard even the simplest maneuvers were to perform correctly.

The class had been an instant success. The makeup of the class has changed over the years as it moved to another rink and finally to *N'ice Skates*. There were men in the club now, and not everyone was a skating parent. I usually skated it myself but sometimes, if Etienne got too involved in management stuff, I got to teach it. I still hadn't decided which was harder—skating it or teaching it. We had gradually added some of the Portugal and Half Moon Bay parents to it as they, too, learned how difficult the feats were that their children were learning.

Of the original group, most were grandparents now. Their children had grown up, quit skating, gone on to college and married. There were always baby showers for the new members of the families.

I had started skating at ten years old on a pond in my home town. It was not until eleven years later that I had any lessons. But skating is addictive. My own personal belief is that it is, for the truly smitten, a disease for which there is no known cure. We just recently had a birthday party for one of the original Coffee Club members. It was special for one thing because the lady announced that she was going to stop skating. She felt that she was just slightly past it. The birthday we were celebrating was her ninety-fifth!

I hoped the meeting wasn't going to take too long. After all the alarms and upsets of the past two days, I needed exercise and skating the class would release a lot of tension.

Etienne started off, "I'm sure you're all aware of the problems we've been having. I think that it important that we keep everything as normal as possible. Berrien, will you tell us how the show is progressing, please?"

Startled, my mind still back in the prehistory of the Coffee Club, I stuttered, "Wha'…what? You want me to talk about the show?"

"That's what I asked."

For this we had to have a special meeting! I could almost see the smoke coming out of various, assorted ears. The weight coach, due at the rink only on Tuesdays, Thursdays and Saturdays was furious. He had nothing to do with the show and had called in sick the day before. At least he hadn't been told yet that I expected him to work backstage, moving props. He was a typical body builder, huge muscles, thick neck, massive legs, only about five feet six inches. He liked to be called by his nickname, Trick. Brewster was his last name. I had no idea what his real name was. He had come to us for work, well recommended by several physical therapists. Trick had some sports development training and was willing to work for the small salary we were paying him in the hope that he would, in the near future, have a full-time job with us and would therefore qualify for one of the coaches cottages that were just now being built. We didn't plan to charge for them as they were really designed for the use of visiting coaches and for someone like Trick, permanent staff but not privately employed.

Ariadne Marsh, the dance instructor, was too ladylike to fume. Her straight back got even straighter, one tiny foot tapped on the floor. From the tempo, it had to be something from *Die Götterdämmerung*. She had been a principal dancer in some of Europe's most prestigious ballet companies. Love brought her to us. She had met and married a United States Army officer stationed in Germany. When he retired from the military to come home to his beloved San Francisco, Ariadne naturally came along. A little too long in the tooth to get on in a strange country as a dancer, she decided to teach. The prospect of working with skaters had excited her and we were more than happy to have her.

I started to describe the show situation. "The music is done for all the production numbers. David has promised to help me do the Russian number. I could use some help with some other choreography, though. Anyone want to volunteer?"

Just at that moment the front door opened and a large dolly was pushed in. There were boxes and boxes piled one on top of another. Behind this moving skyscraper of cardboard was a little man in the familiar brown United Parcel uniform. Following him was Jonathan Martin, Sheriff's deputy.

"You can't bring all that stuff in here. We have to check everything that's brought in," Jonathan said to the gentleman delivering the parcels. "I told you that outside."

"Look, Mac, you do your job and I'll do mine. It says here on this paper I got to deliver this to Berrien Gamble. You told me she was in here. So go find her for me."

The deputy, somewhat put out at being used as a bellhop, opened, then closed his mouth. He looked around and saw us all around Etienne's desk and beckoned to me.

"'Scuse me. I think I am being paged. I bet those are some of the costumes we ordered. What's that about their having to check everything that comes in here? Are they going to bring in a metal detector, too? That's the most ridiculous thing I have ever heard!"

"No. They mean packages, Berrien. There's no telling what's in those boxes."

"Well, I'll go look at the labels. We should be getting some of the shipments by now. We ordered them a couple of months ago."

I went out to talk to the UPS man and Deputy Martin. "What's this? The stuff from the costume stores, I hope."

"Ms. Gamble, we have to look at every package. The FBI told us to."

"Look at these labels. They're all from costume companies. We ordered them for the show. I'm not going to have you all mess these orders up! It's a hard enough job to keep this stuff straight as it is."

"Miss, will you please sign for these? I got to get on to the rest of my customers." This from the delivery guy as he pushed one of those stupid machines under my nose and handed me the special pen that goes with it. I signed it after counting the number of cartons. Twenty-seven, right.

"You aren't going to leave them in the middle of the aisle, are you?"

"We have to look in them before you can touch them, Ms. Gamble. I'll help you move them after I get someone here to help me check everything out."

"Okay, but I'm going to stand here when you do. If they get out of order, my costume ladies are going to hand me my head in a basket! You are doing it today, aren't you? The ladies have to start sewing the extra trim on some of them as soon as possible. Pictures are scheduled in two weeks." So much for teaching or even skating the Coffee Club hour. "Call me when you're ready to start opening the boxes."

I went back to Etienne's office. He was winding up the meeting, having given the rest of the show news himself. Other business was put off until the regular meeting next week. He had gotten an offer of help from Ariadne for choreographing some of the ballet number, which would be a big help, and no doubt, make the number a lot better than I could do.

Chapter 10

Etienne got his skates on to go work the Coffee Club. Since I was unavoidably present and the requested help from the Sheriff's Department hadn't arrived yet, I decided to skate it, too.

We started with stretches, lined up along the rail with one leg on the top board while we bent the rest of our bodies into some mighty peculiar positions. When I teach the class, I do the exercises, but Etienne merely stands in the middle of the ice, yells a lot and laughs at us. Someone once wanted to make a videotape of the class. He barely escaped from the arena with the camera intact.

"All right, everyone. Down to the far end. We are warm enough."

Twenty-seven ladies and three men skated to the far end as commanded by our leader.

"Now, we begin. We will do the bracket step. Right foot first."

Loud groans could be heard from everyone. This step is a particularly punishing move, especially to the members of the class who have never really done school figures. Calves, thighs, waists and shoulders twisted their tortuous way down the two hundred foot length of the ice, arms flailing, muttered words better not understood.

"Now, left foot," said our torturer, standing still on the very spot where Uncle Tomaso had been found.

A commotion began at the front door. I looked up, hoping to see the reinforcements for the package inspection. It was Vaughan Pike coming in with Paul beside him. Pike was dressed in a navy blue suit, pressed to within an inch of its life, a light blue shirt with French cuffs showing under the sleeves of the jacket, polished loafers and the loudest print tie I had ever seen. Having been caught on camera the day before and shown to the world in a ratty old ski sweater, he wasn't taking any chances on a repeat sartorial disaster.

"When Tami is found, you will come back to me. It is not healthy here. A dead man, a kidnapping, the eternal fog. None of this is good for your skating," Vaughan was screeching at Paul.

Paul said something in a low voice that we couldn't hear. Miki and Sheli came out of the music room to see what the noise was all about and Pike saw them. It inflamed him even more.

"You two! You stole my champions. I will complain to the USFSA. I must have them back!" he shouted as he raised his fist and tried to run down the hallway. Paul grabbed him just as he got started and Pike tripped over the pile of packages. "I'll sue, I'll sue!" As he got up, I noticed that he was limping slightly.

Deputy Martin had thrown the door open when he had heard the commotion start and rushed to help the man up. "Now, now. Simmer down. What's all this about?"

The coach turned on him furiously. "Leave me alone. If I want any help from you, I'll ask for it. Let go of me!"

Sheli stood, openmouthed. Used as she was to the strange goings-on in the skating world, this one was beyond peculiar.

Misty, who had been sleeping close to Gillian's candy drawer as usual, heard the voice she hadn't liked the day before and had scratched at the door until Gillian let her out. The dog headed for Pike, growling. I ran off the ice to get her before she did any unprovoked damage to the man.

The members of the Coffee Club, carefully warmed up, were standing around, staring at the wild man, trying to make sense of what was going on. Etienne headed off the ice to confront the pro himself. Fortunately, none of the kids were in the rink, this morning being adults only.

There was a clatter of clogs coming down the stairs as Trick, who had stayed to use the weight room himself, rushed to help with whatever was happening that might need his strength. We had quite a gathering of upset, emotionally-charged and rowdy people. Trick spotted the group close to the door. "Hi, Mr. Pike," he called.

"Everyone calm down," Etienne said. "Suppose we try to find out why Mr. Pike really is here. Deputy Martin, please take him in to my office. Vaughan, do you need a doctor? Did you hurt yourself when you tripped?"

"No. I don't want any hick doctor from around here!"

Paul, Etienne and Deputy Martin more or less surrounded Pike and hustled him into the office.

Miki was standing very close to his sister. She was sobbing. "Sheli, don't worry about what he said. You know, everyone knows, that Paul and Tami chose to come here. Everything will be fine. You'll see. Tomorrow we'll hear from her again. Take it easy."

"What is this all about, anyhow?" asked Trick, still not on the same page as the rest of us.

"Oh, Trick, it's just a mix-up. Vaughan hasn't been quite right recently. He's upset, I guess about Tami being missing. After all, he coached her in singles and then got Paul together with her for pairs. We all get fond of our students, you know," I answered not quite truthfully.

David, who had been on the ice with the dance team arrived to join the happy group. "Wasn't that Vaughan Pike? What's he doing here?"

"Who knows? Worried about Tami, maybe. I wonder who's teaching his kids? I ran into him yesterday at the general store. He was ranting and raving then."

We could see the group in Etienne's office. Their mouths were moving, looking for all the world like a bowl full of goldfish. As we were contemplating this less than appetizing scene, two very young deputies arrived at the rink. Both were tall, slim and good-looking in their smart, silver-grey and light blue uniforms. All their leather equipment, belts, holsters, pepper spray holders and so forth had not a scratch on them. Brand new to police work, I bet. The young man didn't look old enough to be shaving, although given his white-blond hair, a beard probably wouldn't show very much anyway. The girl was almost as tall as the man was with curly, light brown hair escaping the pony tail band she had on.

"Where is Deputy Martin? We're supposed to report to him. We have to search some boxes."

Just then, Jonathan looked out the office window, waved and got up to come out into the rink. "What took you so long? It shouldn't have taken you an hour to get here."

"Sorry, sir. We were over in Redwood City and there was a monster accident on Highway 92. We came over the back roads," replied the young man.

"Okay. Let's get started on these packages. We have to check them for notes or anything unusual. I called the Feds, one of them is on the way, too but they said we could get started."

The two young officers, Nancy Toland and Keith Walker, looked at the stack of boxes, now in disarray after Pike's accident.

"Where do we start?" Nancy wondered out loud.

"First, I go get my skates off, then we three will organize them. Trick, will you please go get the rolling racks in the storage room? There should be several cases of hangers. Bring them, too."

I gathered scissors, hanging tags, several colored pens and a big bag of safety pins when I went to get the skates off. There was the organizational chart for the show, too. If we did, indeed, have to open all those boxes, I was going to make certain that none of the costumes got tops and bottoms mixed up. It was going to be a long day.

By the time I got to the pyramid of boxes, Ariadne had surfaced from the dance studio and Trick had located the clothes racks and wire hangers. The hangers had obviously been doing what they do best, multiplying exponentionally. They were overflowing the cartons and had gotten so tangled that it was going to be a day's work just to get them separated.

Figuring to keep both Ariadne and Trick occupied without letting them handle the costumes yet, I suggested they straighten the pesky metal things out while Nancy and Keith separated the cartons into piles according to manufacturer. Then we could get started.

The biggest number of boxes was from *The Costume Shop*. We all started on those. The first container we opened had twenty pair of men's black stretch trousers in assorted sizes, each sealed in its own plastic bag. Keith started to open one.

"Hold it. If it's in a sealed bag, there can't be anything unusual in it. Let's leave them in their bags," I said.

"Oh, we can't do that. Deputy Martin said we have to open everything."

"Come on. These were obviously packed in a factory. If we open every plastic bag we'll be here until next Wednesday. Go get him out here again. Or better yet, we can open all these boxes and see what's not shrink wrapped, or whatever, then decide. Just *The Costume Shop* boxes, now. And don't get the contents mixed up!"

Nancy and Keith raised their eyebrows, looked at each other and shrugged. If this were their first duty day, they might decide to change career paths.

I could hear the music of the Paso Doble in the background. *España Cani*, long the standard that had made generations of ice-dancers say "Ole" and start off on one of the most fun dances in skating. At one time, a number of years ago, someone had discovered that a song called *The Teddy Bears Picnic* had the right tempo for the Paso and started to use it at dance sessions. Didn't work. Images of teddy bears were not conducive to a fast, Spanish dance. Miki and Sheli were working with a young junior pair team who were showing a lot of promise. The Coffee

Club ladies had finished skating for the day and were chatting away as they packed skates, sweaters and gloves into skate bags, ready to go to lunch, probably somewhere along the Coast.

Mr. Stanley was the lucky FBI agent of the day. He strode into the rink purposefully and stopped, staring at the mess all over the floor. "What the hell is going on here?"

"We're opening all the packages, as you ordered," I answered.

"Only the authorities are supposed to be doing this! And who is he? And her?" he asked pointing toward Ariadne and Trick, who by now were seated on the floor, hopelessly entangled in a mass of wire closely resembling a beach fortification. "Where is Mather? He's supposed to be overseeing this operation."

Deputy Martin came back out of the conference still going on between Etienne, Paul and Vaughan. "Is something wrong, sir? Besides the mess, I mean."

"Have you ever heard of fingerprints, young man? These boxes needed to be checked for prints. Did you do that before you turned these idiots loose on them? Why is everything in those little plastic baggies? We must check everything."

With that, Mr. Stanley picked up a particularly large, opaque bag and yanked it open. Beads of all shapes, types, colors, and sizes flew into the air and cascaded down onto the federal agent. His greying hair was decorated with sequins, bugle beads were spilling down the front of his grey suit and the tiny beads used to hold the trim on were worming their way into his spotless, buffed loafers to remind him of today for weeks to come. When we ordered the costumes, we had ordered a box of mixed trim for when—not if—some fell off. The floor was littered with glitter.

"Oh, get on with it," he muttered as he tried to brush bright red sequins out of his jacket pocket. The pesky things always seemed to stick where they shouldn't and dripped off beautiful costumes where they had been both glued and sewn on.

I started opening bags, and hanging costumes up, sorted by size and by sequence in the show. They were then labeled for individual skaters so that the costume ladies—for that read skating mothers who had been bamboozled into volunteering—could iron everything and sew loose trim on securely. It was slow work doing it alone. Ariadne, extricating herself from the hangers, came over to help.

We worked silently for awhile as the two young deputies continued their careful examination of every bag as it came out of a box. Despite my misgivings, this was really working out quite well. I had to admit we were getting a lot done pretty quickly. The colorful, sparkly costumes hung like limp lingerie on the pipe racks.

Pike came out of the office, then turned back to shake hands with Etienne. He was acting normally now. If anyone could calm him down it would be our manager. Mainly because 'Tienne himself could throw outrageous temper tantrums and did when his charm, which was considerable, didn't work. The coach left the rink just as Mr. Stanley came down the hallway from the rest rooms.

"Hey, Mr. Pike," he shouted, "may I have a word with you?"

"Sure. Goodby. Now you've had two from me."

"No, no. I'd like to ask you a few questions. You know Tami Tompson pretty well, don't you? Has she ever behaved in a funny—I mean peculiar—way before?"

"The only peculiar thing she ever did was to leave me and come to this god-forsaken place. Look at them. Sprawled on the floor opening plastic bags! Did you ever see such a bunch of unprofessional professionals?"

He was becoming agitated again and slammed out the doors, pushing both panic bars as hard as he could. The Fed ran after him and they disappeared from our sight.

'Tienne came out of the office and stood, looking over the costumes. "They are bright, to say the least!" was his only comment. Then, "Since it doesn't look like anybody is going to get out to lunch I've ordered some pizzas. They'll be here soon."

Surprised, I looked down at my watch. It was well past one o'clock. "Okay, that'll be great but no one, repeat no one, is to touch these costumes while eating!"

A few minutes later the delivery man from Amador's, a marvelous Italian restaurant in Half Moon Bay, arrived. He staggered in the door with what looked like more cartons than the UPS guy had brought, except these smelled better, and the FBI wasn't going to need to inspect them.

Wrong. Stanley came barging back in. He was in an even fouler mood than when he had gone out after Pike.

"What's in those boxes?"

"It had better be pizzas. I ordered plenty. Won't you have some?" Etienne asked as he was busy opening the cartons and putting them out on the benches.

Ariadne floated into the office to get a supply of napkins and paper plates. Gillian picked up the portable phone and came out to get her share of the pizza. Poor lady, I expected to see calluses on her ears from all the phone work she had been doing the last couple of days. She brought out some cups and the coffee pot from the office. David had corralled some sodas from the refrigerator in the pros' room.

"We have to look under the food. There may be a message," said Stanley.

"Oh, for God's sake, you have hidden paper on the brain," Etienne replied. "Go ahead, look under them but go wash your hands first."

We all selected a slice of our personal favorite. Mine was the Shrimp Ahoy with shrimp, roasted garlic, plenty of drippy mozzarella cheese, sun-dried tomatoes and a pesto sauce. There were four varieties, and four of each. I didn't see any way all of these would be finished. Oh, well, 'Tienne could put the remainder in his refrigerator upstairs.

The FBI agent came back from the bathroom, drying his hands on paper towels. Then he reached into his jacket pocket and brought out a small tube and squeezed some ointment into the palm of his hands. It smelled powerfully of Calvin Klein for Men.

"Oh, no," yelped David. "If you're really going to paw through these pizzas, get rid of that smelly stuff."

Stanley obligingly wiped most of it away with the damp towels he was still cradling in the crook of his elbow. Then he proceeded to pick up every box and check the underside, after which he lifted each gooey slice in every box to check there, too. He was, at least, thorough. Finally he helped himself to a big slice of the vegetarian one, covered with artichoke hearts, mushrooms, garlic, onions and a tomato basil sauce.

Paul, looking as much like a lost waif as anyone could who was over six feet tall, sank down onto one of the benches. He idly toyed with a slice of the Greek pizza, complete with olives, feta cheese, anchovies and tomatoes. "I'm so upset I'm not even hungry," he mumbled around the big slice. "Do you suppose we'll really see Tami tomorrow? I hope so. Oh, I want her back. It's no fun skating alone anymore. She's always got something funny to say, when one of us falls."

"It's usually you, too," Sheli piped up.

The two young officers were holding their own in the "pizza derby." They had, between the two of them, almost polished off an entire five cheese delicacy. And the temporarily anorectic Paul was finishing the last slice in the box he was holding in his lap.

Talk was minimal, each one of us afraid to start any topic that might lead back to Uncle Tomaso's mysterious appearance and death and the missing Tami. Trick had chosen a slice of the vegetarian pizza and was busy chewing each small bite thirty times. Between the minuscule bits of pizza he went on about health foods.

"You know," the weight trainer lectured, "we really need a juice bar in here. One where we can mix up some good, healthy drinks instead of stuffing ourselves with all this fat."

While he had a point, we all felt that was carrying things too far. It was true that we did have a training restaurant planned to go with the skaters cottages. However, those concoctions that we had seen in the various gyms we had all tried were not among our plans.

"Okay, everyone. Let's clean up this mess and get back to the costume boxes," I urged. "Be sure you wash your hands—Keith, you need to clean that cheese off your arms, too—before you even think of touching the costumes!"

My fussing over the various and sundry leotards, dresses and other bits of cheap decoration must have seemed bordering on the paranoid to my helpers. Only Etienne and David, and possibly Ariadne, could understand. Close up the outfits didn't look at all prepossessing. On human bodies, on the ice (or a stage) with colored spotlights catching the glitter, they would be transformed, as if by magic, bringing the scenes described by the music, to life. Unfortunately, they were not designed for a long life and a washer or dryer would spell their end.

A long time ago, amateur shows used home-grown labor to produce the necessary outfits. Years of working with parents and grandparents to get matching costumes only led to large numbers of ulcers among the pros responsible. Handed patterns, yardage amounts and the name and address of the particular store who had special ordered the fabric and trim necessary, parents invariably located a store that had a sale.

"Well, it looks a lot like the sample." "The orange color looks better on Susie than that yellow." "The sketch showed it wrong. I just put the pocket where it belonged." "I didn't have time to finish it, so it's just pinned."

All were excuses which I have personally heard. The result was always no sleep for a week while my own sewing machine overheated. Which was why I had gone to store-bought costumes and allowed only chosen ladies to add any extra embellishments that we wanted. The fact was that this approach worked and the skaters in any given number didn't look as if they had wandered in from some other show.

Of course, I always allowed the cold spot solos to use their own, more elegantly designed and constructed outfits. It was only in the production numbers that uniformity was necessary.

Trick, by now, had tamed the wire hangers. He had carefully paper-clipped four together and continued until all of the things were subdued—at least for the time being. He then offered to help Keith and Nancy open boxes and vacuum-sealed baggies.

Mr. Stanley was being a big help by standing over each person in turn, making sure that no messages fell out of the cartons and plastic containers.

Nancy was holding up a large plastic bag. It had eight hot pink leotards with black lace ruffles along the leg openings.

"Oh, terrific," I said, "they're the outfits for the Senior Octet. Open it. I want to see them close. The picture wasn't all that great and we need to see how much extra trim has to be added." The group was skating to *Gaite Parisenne.*

She opened the bag and handed them to me one at a time. Two size Small. Two size Medium. Five size Large. "Right," I acknowledged as they were checked off the master list. The extra one was always ordered. Kids tend to grow in four months. I reached for a hanger and opened out the first costume at the same time. Then I looked at this size Large outfit. It was adorable. It wouldn't need any extra trimming. And it was a child's size Large. It wouldn't have fit on the leg of one of the girls in the Senior Octet, the shortest of whom was five feet four inches tall!

Etienne was laughing, a sort of rusty, creaking sound. While he smiled a lot, it was unusual for him to laugh so much. He coughed and, when that stopped, said, "Now you know why I didn't want to produce the show."

Having spent five years in the same rink as 'Tienne where he did do the shows, I had already known. These things happened in the best run shows and now we only had to figure out how to deal with the mini-disaster. I called *The Costume Shop* in Cleveland, Ohio. Of course, they were closed. It was three in California so it would be six o'clock in the East.

Mrs. Simeon was out by the costume racks. She was the mother of one of the girls in the Octet in question. She was also a talented seamstress. She took one look at the costumes and groaned.

"Berrien, the girls can't begin to fit in these things. They are cute, though. Do you think you can get the adult sizes in time for the pictures?"

"I don't know. They're closed now. I'll call again first thing in the morning. If they can't, do you have some time to go to San Francisco with me? We can hit the costume supply stores and dance emporiums—see what they have and what you and your ladies can do."

"I could probably do it Friday. I'll let you know. Now, we'll take all these unpacked ones over to the steamer in the storeroom. They'll look good when we get the wrinkles out."

Mr. Stanley, still standing around, didn't make any objections. "I guess I'll be getting back to the City," he said. "These cartons were all legitimate. We'll have to see what comes next. Oh, Tami's parents are staying in San Francisco. We got them a hotel room there so we can be close to them. Keep us informed of anything new that you hear."

Sean Mather had joined the crew while I was in the office and was sympathizing with Jonathan about the intrusion of the Feds. Meanwhile, he continued, "We still have to figure out what happened to Uncle Tomaso."

"So you don't think his death and Tami's disappearance are connected?" I asked.

"How could they be? One's a guy, hasn't been around his hometown in years, the other's a kidnapping of a sorta celebrity—that is, if you consider a skater a celebrity."

"Gee, thanks for the compliment! By the way, did you get a chance to talk to Jonathan? He's the one who came out to my place last night, or to be accurate, early this morning. I had a prowler of some kind."

"You guys are becoming a whole crime wave here at the rink, all by yourselves, aren't you? No, Jonathan didn't say anything to me. I'll read his report when I go back to the office, though."

"Oh, there's my three o'clock lesson. I'd better get out there. See you later. Marguerita, I'll be right with you. Mrs. Simeon, get Trick to help you take those racks to the storeroom."

I went out to give Marguerita her freestyle lesson and maybe do one or two run-throughs of the show program that we had done the other day.

"Ariadne, can you stay for a few minutes? I want you to see 'Rita's program. We did the basics a couple of days ago but we need some arm positions to finish it off."

"Of course, Berrien. I'd love to help."

The next hour was pure pleasure. Marguerita is a hard worker with a marvelously retentive memory. She went through the *Malagueña* program without a mistake the very first time. Ariadne made some excellent suggestions, setting moves for her arms that worked well and added to the whole presentation. We were all pleased with the results. I got the video camera and taped the last run-through and showed her what she looked like.

Like many serious skaters, 'Rita doesn't like to watch herself skate. She sees flaws where there really aren't any and agonizes over every miss-step.

"Oh, Berrien, I took six steps instead of eight! I must do it again. Please?"

"Okay. One more time. Then we need to get to work on the new jumps. Ariadne, thanks so much. The ballet number rehearses on Friday at five. Can you come then?"

"Of course. Do you have an extra copy of the music so I can study it?"

"Sure, I'll get it as soon as Marguerita does the program one more time. Oh, and thanks for all your help with the costumes today. Sorry you had to come over for such a nothing meeting. Etienne gets excited, sometimes and just doesn't think."

"You're very welcome for the help. It makes me feel useful. And don't worry about the meeting. You forget, I'm European and used to types like Mr. Lepardeiux. I'll see you Friday."

CHAPTER 11

It had been a long, tiring day. I went out of the rink with Misty, who had spent another hour or so after the pizza lunch resting. Personally, I had made a pig of myself on the stuff and didn't want any dinner. However, I remembered the sad state of the refrigerator and freezer so we headed on into Half Moon Bay to Safeway for some major shopping.

The weather was gorgeous, as only an early April day on the Coast can be. I could see the ever-present fog on the horizon with its promise of a very cool night, but for the present the sun was shining. The brilliant light moved with each wave as we rode along the highway. Sea birds were pottering along the edge of the continent, searching for their next tasty morsel. I watched two large brown pelicans dive down, stick their great beaks under the water and soar again into the air, dinner wriggling in their giant beaks.

Oleander and lavender were blooming along the roadside. The scattered houses had an almost infinite variety of trees, from stately palms to tall, handsome evergreens. The area had many Christmas tree farms. Philip, Trent and I had come over to Half Moon Bay every year when we lived on the Peninsula to cut our own tree. They always smelled so good. It seemed as if the trees trapped their own woodsy scent along with capturing the sea-smell of the ocean in their fine needles.

Misty Joy stuck her nose out the window. I never opened the window too far. She had gotten an ear infection when she was a puppy and ever since then always had problems with her ear. The breezes stirred by fifty mile an hour speeds would invariably bring on an infection but she could get her long pointed nose out pretty far.

The town seemed crowded, especially so close to dinner time in the middle of the week. Then I noticed that the parking lots at the hotels, motels and bed and breakfast inns were all full. The vans and trucks of the media had, indeed, left the arena parking lot but they hadn't retreated far away. They were in town, waiting to see what would happen the next morning.

As I pulled into the Safeway parking lot a group of reporters was headed to a restaurant nearby. One tall young man spotted me, well, actually Misty Joy. There aren't very many pure white dogs who sit up as high in the car as she does. I knew it wouldn't be me.

I'm sort of non-descript. Late forties, fairly fit because of the skating and even more so because of Etienne's habit of drafting me to skate precision rehearsals. He uses me and Sheli to fill in, in both the junior and senior teams, whenever a girl is out. If I ever stop skating, though, I will have to give up large helpings of pizza or I will get hugely fat. Even with all the exercise, I have never been confused with Twiggy.

My hair is sort of brown, what my father called dun-duckety mud color, wavy rather than curly and given to going in several directions at once. It has been almost every color of the rainbow, long before punk was punk. Platinum blond through raven black (what a disaster that was) with all shades in between. Now I have decided to leave it alone. The grey is beginning to show here and there. I quite like it…sort of nature's own frosting.

For years I have tried to work on my carriage, loving the way David looks both on and off the ice. As a result, I have a good straight back, as most skaters do, but my knees and hips have never cooperated in my attempts at gliding across a room.

The life-long love affair I have had with skating has been fraught with difficulty, despair and delight, not always in equal portions. It has been my passion. While talented to a certain extent, I have been more a solid, workman-like skater. Maybe that's why I liked, respected and understood Brandi, although she skated because her mother insisted, not from passion for the sport.

My school figures were good. They take patience, willingness to repeat a move endlessly and lots of time. My freestyle skating was another story. The spins were easy to learn and do, footwork was fun and I had spirals that were wonderful—at least so I was told. However, my jumps were pitiful. I once told a pro that the jumps were so hard for me because I was afraid of heights. His answer was swift. "You don't need to worry. You don't get that high."

I could see the group of reporters headed our way. In their number was Vaughan Pike. Why was he with them I wondered? Maybe he was hoping to get the latest news on Tami first. It was still a mystery as to why he was hanging around. His erratic behavior was becoming more pronounced and the media people were sure to notice, if they hadn't already.

Now was a good time to sit in the car and make a list. I grabbed some paper from the floor and started in. After listing about fifty items, I gave up. It would be easier just to go get one of everything.

It was hard to ignore ten grown men, all clustered around the car, but I did my best as I stepped out onto the macadam.

"Berrien, what's the latest?" "Have you heard anything new?" "Come on, tell us what's going on." I was barraged with questions on all sides. Then suddenly, strong hands were grabbing at my throat. Misty, locked in the car, was going bananas, scratching at the windows, trying to get her paws through the small opening I had left her, yelping her surprising, loud, frantic bark.

Vaughan Pike was again, for the second time in two days, after me. Flashbulbs were popping all around us. One of the reporters finally, after what seemed a lifetime, tried to pull Pike away. Pike was screaming unintelligibly, saliva running down his chin. Through the grey haze that was descending on me, I could hear other voices, felt hands pulling me one way while the body that had been so close to me was forced farther away. His hands were still wrapped around my neck. Finally, he shrieked, let go of me and collapsed in a heap at my feet. Strong, slim arms were holding me up.

I turned my head carefully and could see Sheli alongside me. Now she was yelling at Pike who was still in an untidy heap on the ground, sobbing in frustration. Mrs. Andrade, right behind Sheli, was adding her voice to the general bedlam as more pictures were taken of the fracas.

The store manager rushed out. "Berrien, shall I call a doctor? Are you okay?"

Ted Ruthen, a print reporter for the San Francisco Chronicle said, "Yes, get a doctor but call the cops, too. Pike just tried to kill her!"

I tried to speak but couldn't. Tried again and managed to croak, "No, no police. I'll be all right but he might need a doctor." I gestured toward the heap. "A padded cell probably wouldn't be unreasonable, either."

Sheli still had a firm grip on one of my arms. Pike was holding his left hand and moaning. I knew then what had happened. Sheli had broken his fingers to make him let go of me. What a mess! Thank heaven there had been no television people around.

I shook her off and opened the car door so Misty could see that I was okay. Once reassured, her barking stopped. She gave me a great big kiss and I winced. She had gotten my neck. It was really going to be sore.

The store manager was dithering. Was this good for business or bad? The ambulance from Carmichael Hospital arrived in minutes, and two paramedics hurried over to the cluster of people milling around my car.

Mrs. Andrade had gotten the manager to supply me with some bottled water and I gulped it down past the bruises that were already forming around my neck.

"She broke my hand. I want to report her! Get the police," screamed the skating coach, pointing at me!

"No, she didn't. I did and I'm glad I did," Sheli said. "I don't know what you're doing hanging around here for anyway. Go back to the students you still have left. If you get your picture in the paper anymore doing these crazy things, no one is going to allow their kids to stay with you. What's wrong with you?"

The media people were eating this scene up. Rumors were the norm in such an egocentric sport as skating but the events of the past few days were not gossip but the real thing. There were feature writers with the group now, not just sports jocks.

The paramedics looked at me and I shook my head, carefully, slowly. "I'll be all right. Just bruises. And scared." I turned to Sheli. "Boy, am I glad you arrived. Thanks."

"Don't mention it. Do you want help driving home? Mom can take my car and I'll drive you."

"I've got to get some groceries. I'm even out of milk and eggs. Do you have time to wait?"

"Of course. Mom, come with us. I'm not leaving you out here with these reporters. You've already said more than enough for them to quote."

The young paramedic who had been first on the scene at the rink when we had found Uncle Tomaso came over to us. He had examined Pike's hand.

"What did you hit his hand with, Sheli? He's got about seven broken bones! We can't tell for sure 'til we get it X-rayed but that hand's a mess!"

"I just used my hands, bent the fingers backward. He didn't want to let go of Berrien so didn't try to stop me. He should have known better. He's the one that taught me that trick!"

Pike was loaded, moaning loudly and dramatically, into the ambulance and it headed back up the highway. Sheli, Mrs. Andrade and I went in to the store. We took carts and agreed to meet at the checkout counter. I headed for the ice cream. I had a feeling that's what I was going to be eating for the next several days.

By the time we met back at the front of the store my voice had gone again. To say nothing of wanting to scream every time I swallowed. But that would have hurt too much. There was still quite a crowd in the parking lot, enlarged by two Sheriff's cruisers. Damn! I was in no shape to meet yet more of the county's finest. All I wanted to do was get home and open the first half gallon of raspberry swirl ice cream.

As we all left the store, one of the deputies left the group and walked purposefully over to us. It was Mather. Again.

"I need to get details. Shall we start now?"

"Deputy Mather," I whispered, "could you possibly come to my house? We've got frozen stuff here and I honestly need to sit down. Sheli's going to drive me home so we'll both be there. Just follow us."

"Well, okay. I'll leave the other guys here to get the story from these witnesses. I've sent another man out to the hospital to hear Mr. Pike's side of the story."

"That ought to be interesting," Sheli said as she loaded their groceries in the Cherokee. "Mom, take this stuff on home. The deputy doesn't need all of us and that frozen food will defrost soon."

"How'll you get home?"

"I'll call Miki. He's still at the rink with David. We invited him over for dinner. Poor guy is shook-up in spades."

Mrs. Andrade left and Sheli and I piled groceries into the trunk of my car. Sheli got in the driver's seat while I collapsed into the back seat. Misty Joy allowed no one in her seat. She, I believe, felt that only she could navigate from here to there properly. I realized that I was still shaking. My hands fumbled in my bag for a cigarette, forgetting that I had quit more than three years ago. Just as well, I probably would have singed my bangs with the lighter, anyhow, with my unsteady hands.

When we arrived home the deputy insisted on checking the house before we went in, then helped us unload the large supply of groceries and miscellaneous necessities I had bought. We put the perishables away and I made some coffee and offered to share some ice cream. Neither Sheli nor Mather took me up on the dessert.

Finally, seated comfortably in the family room with Misty curled up on my lap, and most of the rest of the couch, too, the deputy became all business.

"Now, I want to know what the hell is going on with you people. The old man's murder, for murder it was, the kidnapping and now this attack on you, Ms. Gamble. What's next? Is all this a publicity stunt to attract new students? Are you paying this Pike person, whoever he may be? And where is Tami Tompson? Do you guys really not know?"

Both Sheli and I sat there speechless, and not only because of my aching throat.

"That's ridiculous," I squeaked. "Why would we ever want all this mess? None of us would want anything to go wrong. We need national notice—sure, but this kind of farce is more likely to do us a lot of harm. We're looking for parents to want to send their skaters here. Good location, serious skating along with a good education is what we are providing and want to keep on improving on. The kind of trash being written now will only hurt us! It's not going to do much for the town, either, so I can't see anyone in the area pulling these stunts. Of course, Uncle Tomaso's death may have been a prank gone terribly wrong, but the rest of the stuff.... No, we sure wouldn't have anything to do with such nonsense."

My voice got weaker with every word while I was still seething mentally, I had to shut up though because I couldn't even hear myself.

Sheli picked it up. "Do you know anything more about what happened to Uncle Tomaso? Obviously, the family wasn't close to him but we'd like to know what brought him back to town. And naturally, we want you to find out who killed him."

"Well, Ms. Andrade, we only know what we've already told you about his death. He was killed outside the rink and then dragged in later. Whoever killed him probably put him on the ice either as some sort of morbid joke or maybe to confuse the time of death. We don't know about that yet. Or maybe even for the bizarre publicity you're getting. Do you two have any notion of someone who hates one or all of you enough to try to close the arena?"

Half of my large bowl of ice cream was gone and the cold and smoothness had done its work, even if only for a short time. "Only Pike, as far as I know. He's furious because Paul and Tami came here to Miki and Sheli. He feels, I guess, that they are his. He's always had something of a temper but, as far as I know, his students always got along with him until recently."

"Yes, Sean—you don't mind, do you? After all, we went to high school together. Paul's told us about Vaughan's recent behavior. He says it was really totally unlike him. That's why they left. They weren't comfortable with him anymore. Didn't know when—not if, but when—he was going to explode. Sometimes he tried to poke Paul with a hockey stick to get him to straighten up. Twice he did it when Tami was in the air in a lift! That's not just peculiar but downright dangerous!"

"Any students or parents unhappy with any of you?"

Sheli and I looked at each other and shrugged simultaneously. Then I said, "Not that we know of. There's always rivalry in any sport but so far, Tami and Paul are the only international figures we have here. We just got started. I'm having some words with Juliet Taggert about Brandi's costume for the show but even that started after Uncle Tomaso was found. And I think that the people in Portugal are all in favor of us now. Even the ones who were so dead set against us at first. We try to be good neighbors."

"Okay. One of the problems we are trying to figure out is how anyone got into the rink after Miki locked it. The front door doesn't look as if it had been tampered with at all. Is Miki sure he locked it?"

"I watched him, Sean. He not only locked it but even jiggled it a couple of times. He's a sort of compulsive when it comes to locking things up. There's no way anyone could have gotten in. I even remember him checking the lock on the Zamboni room doors, both the outside and the inside."

"What do you mean 'outside and inside'?"

"Oh, we always keep those doors open when people are in the rink. The fuel is kept outside, of course, and you never know when the darned things are going to run out of propane, so we just keep both doors open so we can get to it more easily."

"You mean that sort of garage door was open when you two were teaching Tami and Paul?"

"Sure. Any rink I've ever been in, those doors are open if the weather isn't absolutely impossible outside. Isn't that so, Berrien?"

"Come to think of it, you're right. I know Etienne insists that they be open. He claims it's safer because if there's any kind of fire, he can get the machines out of the building before anything can explode."

Mather sat back and sipped his coffee. He was mulling that information over.

"Is there anyway someone could have slipped into the rink while you were teaching, Sheli?"

"Well, sure, I guess. We were concentrating on the team, acting as spotters, too, for the new lift we invented for them. And of course, we had them run through their new encore program a couple of times so I was playing the music, my back would have been to the Zamboni room and Miki was skating around with them. He wouldn't have been looking at anything besides them."

"Any other time someone could have come in?"

"I don't think so. The skate guards check the rest rooms after public session is over and the second floor rooms all lock. We don't want any young kid getting in the weight room or the dance studio. We have a trampoline in the dance room. Kids could get hurt if they played in either place," Sheli tallied.

"And the storeroom and first aid room are always locked and so is the pros' room and the music library," I added. "About the only place anyone could hide would be the public rest rooms or maybe ducked down behind the skate counter. But Sheli would have probably seen anyone getting in there."

"Would Miki have checked the rest rooms, do you think?"

"No. There'd be no reason to. The skaters have their own changing rooms so Paul and Tami would have said something if there had been a stranger in either of them. And both Miki and I saw them both get in Paul's car before we left, while Miki was locking the front door."

"Okay. It seems possible, if highly improbable, that someone could have gotten into the rink before you all left. Right?"

"Sure. Possible but why?" Sheli wanted to know.

"I haven't any idea yet. Kids do the strangest things sometimes, just on a dare. Or maybe it was one of those guys who go around spray-painting their messages all over the countryside."

"But there wasn't anything painted anywhere. Did you find any paint cans or anything?"

"No. Just an idea. But it still seems a strange coincidence that a body turns up at the rink and sometime that same day a skater gets kidnapped. I think they have to be connected," Mather said, talking more to himself than to us.

He started talking again. "What do either of you know about your employees? What kind of checks do you run on them? How about the skate guards? I know you hired as many local kids as possible. Even taught them how to skate so they could work at the rink. What about the ones who aren't local? And that muscle-bound Arnold Schwartzenegger, junior grade—where'd he come from?"

"Don't you want to know about Ariadne, too?" I asked.

"No. She's a foreigner, and not a skater. This is something about skating. I can feel it."

"Feel it! I didn't think cops felt things. I thought only facts interested you guys. Oh, wait a minute. There was one funny thing today. Earlier, when Pike came into the arena, Trick was coming down the stairs. He said hello to Vaughan, as if he knew him. I didn't think anything about it. But Trick is from around here, or at least he's from northern California someplace. He had good recommendations, too. I'm sure Etienne checked them out. We needed someone who knew how to train skaters."

"Maybe I'd better check him out. That Pike sure is a strange one, isn't he? Has he always been so temperamental? Why did he attack you tonight, Berrien?"

"Damned if I know. I got out of the car and he headed straight for me. He did the same thing earlier in the day at the rink—headed for Sheli—but he tripped over the stack of boxes everyone was searching through. That's when Trick spoke to him but I don't remember Vaughan saying anything to him. Paul and Tami have told us about these rages. That's one of the reasons why they left him. I think he must be sick in the head. If he's mad at Sheli and Miki, okay. They have his prize students. But why me? I haven't the faintest idea but it sure seems like the sight of me set him off. He's the one who caused all the hoopla yesterday in Portugal and landed us both on the national news."

Sheli spoke up. "He didn't use to be like that. Oh, sure, he lost his temper every once in a while. But that was at mistakes in skating. We really enjoyed our time with him. We were actually sorry when Mom got in an argument with him and moved us to another coach. She was always doing that, you know."

"May I use your phone? We'd better call the hospital and see how he's doing. By the way, are you going to file charges against him? From what I heard from those reporters, they thought he was really trying to kill you."

"I thought so, too. Not only trying, but making a real good job of it, until Sheli got there. I don't know about charges, though. I'd sure like to know why he heads for me, I really don't want it to keep happening. I've never done anything to him, but filing charges? It seems that maybe he's sick and needs help more than jail time. Let me think about it."

Mather called the hospital emergency department. "Deputy Mather here. I'm calling to check on a man who came in earlier tonight with an injured hand. Name's Vaughan Pike. May I speak to the doctor, please? Thanks." Then to us, "She's getting Doctor Huang."

"Yes, doctor. I'd like to know how Vaughan Pike is. Is he still at the hospital?"

A short pause while Doctor Huang answered.

"What do you mean, he's in the operating room? What for?"

Sheli and I looked at each other. Couldn't they set a couple of broken fingers in an office?

"He had a heart attack! While he was in the emergency room. I see. Thank you, Doctor." He turned to us. "You heard, I guess. Well, at least he won't be threatening you for awhile, Berrien. I'll stop by the hospital tomorrow to see how he's doing and keep you all up to date. Good night, now."

I asked Sheli, "Does he have any family? I've never seen him at competitions with anyone but his skaters."

"No, unless he has some in Canada. I think he's originally from there. Maybe we ought to call Etienne. He might know."

"That's a good idea." I got up and went to the phone. The answering machine light was blinking and the number counter showed nine messages. Well, I wasn't going to listen to them for the time being. I dialled 'Tienne's private number.

"Allo."

"Etienne. Pike is in Carmichael Hospital. He had a heart attack and they are operating on him now. Do you know if he has a family? Sheli's with me and she doesn't know. Is he from Canada? Or do you think you should call his rink?"

"No, he's not from Canada. I sure don't know of any family either but I'll call the arena and let them know what happened. 'Night."

I turned to Sheli, who was getting up. A car horn had just honked outside. It had to be Miki. "I'd better get home before Mom shows up on your doorstep looking for me. Take care of yourself. Get some rest. I wonder if putting ice on your throat will help the bruises? Why don't you try it? I'll go get a plastic bag full now."

"No, thanks. I've got to get Misty's dinner and spend some time with her. She was really upset when Pike tried to hurt me and she couldn't get out of the car. And there's all those messages on the machine. I'd love to just erase them without even listening to them but I'd better not. I'll see you tomorrow. Thanks again."

She left and I returned to the answering machine to get the missives. The first was predictably from Philip. Why he never is able to remember time changes was beyond me. At least, he gave me a definite time for his next call. Again, I thanked the powers that be for the absence of television crews at the Safeway.

The next two were the ear-splitting screech of someone's fax machine dialling the wrong number. The fourth was a call from son Trent. As a senior in medical school, due to graduate in less than two months, he didn't get to watch much TV or read anything more than abstruse medical journals so he was a little late with the news. I would call him back when my voice ceased sounding like a rasp file rubbing against a piece of sheet metal.

Trent was well on his way to becoming an orthopedist, his heart's desire. Like all pros, I had put him on skates. Just like his father before him, he absolutely could not learn to skate. Philip had tried. And tried.

And tried for an entire year, three times a week. We even bought him custom-made skates. He is the only person I have ever seen able to fall from the desired vertical position to a definitely undesirable horizontal position without ever bending his knees. Since we were skating at Iceland in Berkeley at the time, his falls registered on the local seismograph as minor earthquakes! Trent did the same, albeit since he was a lot smaller at the age of five, he didn't set off the earthquake detectors. However, he had always been fascinated by the gyrations I went through when on crutches, in casts on various limbs and slings holding assorted body parts in place after my own encounters with the ice. He had decided that he could make his fortune as a doctor to skaters.

The remaining five messages were from reporters wanting interviews. One man had obviously followed the ambulance to the hospital and knew about Pike's heart attack. The next day was going to be nasty.

I went back to the kitchen and fed Misty Joy. She was still upset. It was easy to tell. Her usual method of eating resembled nothing so much as a vacuum cleaner. She had to be bribed with some fresh turkey breast sprinkled on her kibble. I grabbed another bowl of ice cream and we were both quiet for a few minutes.

After checking all the locks on doors and windows, I put all of the outside lights on and we went to the bedroom. I finally looked at my throat. What a mess! Thumb prints on the front of my neck and finger-sized bruises spread around to the back. I started to shake again.

When I went back to the bedroom after a quick shower, the dog was curled up on the bed, unasked. I got in and pulled up the covers, then hugged her ferociously. This poor, gentle soul was as upset in her way as I was. Never, in her whole life, had she been subjected to so many shocks as she had had over the last three days. We fell asleep, cuddled together, one of her giant paws resting on my shoulder.

Chapter 12

A loud groan woke me up. The sun was struggling through a veil of fog. Misty was still curled up on the bed. I looked around wondering where the noise had come from. Then I swallowed and realized it had been me.

We were supposed to hear more about Tami this morning. I grabbed the remote and turned the television set on and channel-surfed until I got a local station. No luck there so I went on to CNN and left it on for awhile. Nothing there, either.

Restless, I got up and made some coffee. Eating anything solid was out of the question so I had another bowl of raspberry swirl ice cream and turned the family room TV on. Still nothing. Maybe I had missed it, but I was sure that someone from the rink would have called me if there were any news.

The non-perishable groceries were still scattered about the kitchen. I puttered around putting them away, switched the channel back to a local station and got another cup of coffee. Misty stood at the door, her polite way of telling me she wanted to go outside. We both stepped onto the large deck, she to tend to her morning duties and I to enjoy the view.

As it always does, the sight, smell and sound of the ocean calmed me down. The television was still on in the family room. I could hear the announcer's voice but couldn't make out what he was saying. Soothed, I went back inside just as he said, "We have just received a tape of the kidnapped ice skater, Tami Tompson. You will remember that the first tape was delivered to CNN on Tuesday morning and there was another tape promised for today. We now have it. We have called the FBI and will be able to show the video shortly."

I sat down on the couch to watch. Two and a half minutes of commercials followed. "Come on, come on!" I muttered.

The announcer returned to the screen. "We're sorry for the delay but we had to call the folks at *N'ice Skates* to make sure they were watching. Now, here it is." With that the screen showed a very visibly distraught Tami, apparently unharmed physically, holding up a local morning newspaper showing today's date, an old but reliable method of proving the continued health of the victim.

"I am instructed to say that I am fine, which is true. I am also told to say that the necessary arrangements for my release are temporarily delayed and that there will be further communication on Sunday," she read from a paper in front of her.

The announcer popped back into view. "That's all. We will, of course, keep you informed as time goes on. There is a breaking story in San Jose and we go now to…" I switched the thing off.

What the devil did the kidnapper mean "temporary delay?" The phone rang. "Hi, Etienne."

"How did you know it was me?"

"You must have seen the announcement. I knew you'd call right away."

"What are we going to do?"

"There's nothing we can do, 'Tienne. It's not a job for skating pros to tackle. We have to trust the FBI and the police to do their jobs. Try to calm down. I'll see you in a little while."

I pulled into the parking lot at the rink about two hours later. It was looking like a metal forest again. Reporters with microphones apparently glued to their fingers waved them in front of me. I shook my head and plowed on, letting Misty intimidate everyone into giving me a clear path to the door. One particularly obnoxious woman almost knocked my teeth out with her mike. I stood on the top step and turned around. Then I pulled the silk scarf from around my neck to show the multi-colored bruises. The media people gasped. At that I whispered, in a much fainter voice than I actually had, "Sorry, no interview. Can't talk."

The front door closed behind me and I heaved a sigh of relief. Etienne was standing at the door to the office. "What was that all about?"

"Oh, I just showed off my beautiful neck and told them I'd lost my voice. Good excuse."

"Let me see it. Are you sure you should be here? Did you go to the doctor? No, of course not. I know better than to even ask you that."

"Did you find out about Pike's relatives? And have you called the hospital to find out how he's doing?"

"No one at his rink knows of any family. The manager was going to go to his house today to see if he can locate any information, then he'll call us back. He also said that Vaughan had been gone for a week and that he hadn't told any of his students where he was going or when he was coming back."

"This gets stranger and stranger."

Gillian called out, "Etienne, telephone. It's that manager at Pike's arena."

"Okay. I'll get it in my office. Come on, Berrien. Let's hear what he has to say. I'll put it on the speaker so you can talk, too." He picked up the phone, "'Allo, Etienne here. One of the pros is here, too. Have you learned anything more?"

"Good afternoon, Etienne. Not much, really. There's nobody at Pike's home and none of the neighbors have a key. I've called our local police and a locksmith. We'll all meet there later today. I told them about his being in the hospital and everything. I'll call you back when I know any more. Have you heard how he's doing?"

"No, but I'm going to call after we've finished talking."

I leaned toward the speaker. "Has he been acting strangely at the arena? Violent? Anything like that?"

"No," came the distorted voice over the miniature speaker, "he's not been violent, at least not when I've been around. Some of his kids aren't happy with him, though. They say their new music doesn't sound right or it's not their type or something and they really are not pleased that he's disappeared. Well, not disappeared, exactly, since we all saw him on television the other day but he's not here. Some of the parents are very upset, too. Why? Has he done anything more than grab that pro's arm?"

"I'm that pro and yes, yesterday afternoon he tried to choke me to death. It was right after that when he had the heart attack."

"Oh, I see. No, he hasn't tried anything like that around here. I'm sure I would have all sorts of furious parents calling me if he had done something that outrageous."

"Well, thanks for the call, we'll be waiting for one from you later. Oh, he's in Carmichael Hospital, in case you need to call to give them insurance information. 'By for now," Etienne said as he hung up. He checked a number in his Roledex and dialled again.

"Carmichael Hospital, good morning," said a chirpy, female voice.

"Er, yes, I wonder if I could speak to one of your patients, please. Name's Vaughan Pike."

The chirpy voice got very serious. "I'm sorry. Mr. Pike is in the Cardiac Care Unit. He can't receive any calls. May I put you through to the nurses' station there?"

"Yes, please."

"CCU. Ms. Nelson. May I help you?"

"I'm Etienne Lepardieux of *N'ice Skates*, in Portugal. I am calling to inquire about Mr. Vaughan Pike," said 'Tienne in English but very formal English. "How is he doing? May he have visitors?"

"Are you family?" the nurse asked.

"No. In fact, we don't know if he has any family. We know him, of course, but no one even at his home rink knows who to notify of his illness. Is he conscious? Able to talk?"

"Well, he is conscious but he has tubes all over. It's hard for him to speak and he's still heavily sedated. The doctors think he will recover, though. Perhaps I should have Doctor Givens call you. Then he might allow you to see him in a day or two."

"That would be fine. Thank you."

"What a mess," I said. "How can someone be that alone? No wonder he's gone off the rails a bit. I think, though, that it better be just you who goes to see him. The sight of me, and Sheli and Miki just infuriate him. Sheli and Miki I could understand but I sure don't know what I've done to him."

Suddenly there was a loud thump above our heads. The weight room was up there. We looked at each other and then raced out of the office and up the stairs. Trick was standing by some free weights with a dumb-founded expression on his good-looking face. He had obviously been working out himself. His whole body was covered with sweat and his hands and arms were covered with chalk. He was steadily swearing, not inventively, but thoroughly, cursing the equipment, the weather and his antecedents.

"Trick, what in the world is going on?" asked 'Tienne.

"The weights fell."

"I can see that. You mean you dropped them?"

"Yes."

"Why don't you pick them up? Is it necessary for you to stare at them? We really can't have that kind of language around here. I know the children can hear it at home or school, but they are not going to hear it in my rink," Etienne thundered.

"Sorry, Etienne. I'll remember. It's just that there's so much stuff going on around here. I'm all upset. And I was late this morning. My car broke down so I missed two workouts with kids. Everything's just a mess!"

"Okay, Trick. Calm down," said that paragon of calmness who reverted to his native language when in a tizzy. "Do you have more appointments today? Or would you like to go home?"

"I've got one with Paul and Tami—oh, no. Tami's not here. I wonder if Paul wants one on his own," he wondered as he ran his chalky hands through his dirty blond hair. "And one with three of the younger kids for some light workouts after school. Maybe I'll just go get some lunch and try to calm down. Maybe in Half Moon Bay."

"We'll see you later, then. Call Paul and see if he wants to come in then go on. Oh, and don't talk to any of those reporters."

"No, sir. I don't want anything to do with them."

"Good."

We all went back downstairs. Trick and Etienne went into the office and I headed to the music room to finish the Junior Octet number and two more cold spot solos. Then the music for the show would be finished. And maybe, if I had time I could work on some of next season's competition music. Not only for my own students but for David's and Miki and Sheli's. I loved finding the best music for individual skaters and was good at it. As a result, I was the pro who usually did most of the competitors' programs.

At *N'ice Skates* we all worked well together. Most of us had known each other for years and we avoided the backbiting and general nastiness that was frequently prevalent at other rinks. We helped each other out and used our combined talents very well. These unusual attitudes were what we hoped would make us, eventually, a truly great training center. Our cooperation was not so strange though when one considered that we, the coaches, owned the complex (well, us and several banks) and its success was vitally important to our own financial health.

I remembered hearing some television show theme songs not too long ago. There had been a popular show a number of years ago called *Eight is Enough* and I thought that music would make a cute octet number. Rooting around in the record section of the vast tape, CD and record library I found the song. It only took fifteen minutes to tape it. Kenny Rogers' *Lady* supplied one solo and for a young, very talented nine-year-old I used *Some Day My Prince Will Come*. I had an idea for that one which would make it one of the surprise hits of the show, while managing to infringe on not one but two companies' copyrighted characters.

My stomach was rebelling at the lack of food. My throat said, "No way." The *Boat Dock* was the answer with another serving of the crab bisque, minus the garlic bread unless it was thoroughly soaked in the soup. Gathering up the new tapes and their duplicates I headed for the office, Misty wagging her tail behind me.

The ice surfaces were almost empty. David was out with the dance team again, this time working on the Killian. That is a apt name for that dance. The steps are simple, except for one sequence. The speed is—well—speedy. I had once found myself the proud possessor of a perfect imprint of my partner's house key on my left hip after we fell. I had landed on my right hip and he had landed on my left hip with his keys in his pocket. After that I made sure my partners were dancing *sans* keys!

A few adults were skating around on the second rink and Paul was there, working on footwork. It usually took him a long time to learn it while Tami, who was a high test ice dancer, picked it up fairly quickly.

There was a gate open. Misty spotted it and ignoring me as I squawked, "No, Misty!" sailed out to meet Paul. Used to this unorthodox skater, he laughed, for the first time in days and picked her up, all ninety pounds of her, and brought her back to me.

Gillian was still on the phone and Etienne was in the office talking again to Mr. Stanley. I guess FBI agents don't have first names. At least we had not yet learned even one of the three agents involved with us.

"Come on in, Berrien," called Etienne. "Mr. Stanley has some small morsels of information he is willing to share with us." Then to the snappily-dressed man sitting in a too-small chair opposite him, "Okay, what did you learn that you can tell us?"

Stanley started to talk. "We know that the tape was hand-delivered to the television station. By a man. About thirty minutes before it was announced on the air. We got over there and ran it before it was shown. You never know. We might have had to edit it some for public consumption. It was all right so we showed the whole thing. After that we took it back to the office and ran some tests on it. We couldn't do a whole lot, we sent it back to D.C. already to get them to work on it. She's getting pretty spooked, but then who can blame her? It really was a morning edition of the paper, not only that but not the one they put out late at night but one printed about six this morning. We think we got some background sounds, especially a fog horn, and a ding-a-ling noise like the cable cars make. We'll know for sure when the lab gets a chance with the tape but it looks like she is somewhere in San Francisco along one of the cable car lines and fairly near the water. That's about all we know. Oh, Mrs. Tompson confirmed that it really was Tami, not someone made up to look like her which is always a possibility."

"How are the Tompsons doing?" I asked. "If they would like to move from the hotel, we could put them up at our place. They might like to be here with the other skaters, especially Paul."

"I'll ask them. They just might like that. I guess I'd better be going. I called the hospital and am going to try to see this Mr. Pike. When are his family arriving, do you know?"

"We can't find any family or even anyone who knows if he has family," Etienne said. He then related what efforts we were making. "Maybe your office should see what they can find out. The story of his heart attack was on the radio last night and the TV news this morning. But thank goodness they didn't make a big scene about his choking Berrien!"

"What do you mean, he choked her?"

I unwound the colorful scarf once again to show the even more gaudy bruises.

"Did you have him arrested? Do the Sheriff's people know about this?"

"Yes, Deputy Mather knows. No, we didn't have him arrested. At least not yet. We will only if necessary. He had the heart attack at the hospital while he was being treated for a couple of broken fingers."

"How, I truly hesitate to ask, did he get his fingers broken?"

"Sheli came up while he had his hands around my neck. He wouldn't let go so she broke his hands."

"Just like that, huh? A young lady goes up to a man considerably larger than she is and breaks his hands. Unbelievable!"

"Oh, no. Remember, Sheli is a pair skater. She has to have strong hands herself as well as Miki. He can't do all the holding. A pair is truly a team. They have to work together."

"After this case, as weird as it is, is over, I'll never make fun of skaters again. I think I'd rather be a quarterback for any major football team before being a skater."

"Well, this is the first time anyone has ever tried to kill one of us. At least that I know of. If you'd like to learn a little bit, come back after you've seen Pike and 'Tienne will give you lesson number one," I joked. "Oh, Etienne, remember we need really good ice tomorrow. The judges are coming over to critique the kids who're taking tests next week. I think they're due at one. Will you make the ice for it, please?"

Even with the Zamboni, ice-making can be tricky. This is particularly true for figure tests where every small blemish in the ice can cause a skater to wobble at a critical time. The tracing on the ice would show a flat, which means skating on both the inside and outside edge at the same time, a no-no, or worse yet a change of edge where the blade flips from the outside to the inside edge or vice versa, even more of a no-no. Etienne knew all of this and would take almost infinite pains with the ice surface. He always made it for tests but this was the first time judges had agreed to come "over the hill" to talk to the skaters and give them some pre-testing help. It was important that we had everything perfect.

"Of course I'll make it. We'll start at Noon and then check it out. Is everything else ready?"

"I hope so. I brought the silver tea service in yesterday and ordered the sandwiches and cakes from the *Tea Party* last week. Maybe I'd better call and check on them. Mrs. Petty said they'd deliver everything at two thirty. That ought to give us enough time."

Not only were we going to have the judges at the arena but they would be meeting the officers of the newly formed provisional skating club for the first time. We had all named it, naturally, *N'ice Skates Club*, and had been happily surprised when the all-powerful United States Figure Skating Association had accepted the name.

Thinking of food, my stomach began to make rude noises. "Would you two like to repair to the *Boat Dock* for some lunch? I haven't eaten since those pizzas yesterday except for some ice cream. I think maybe I could go for some soup."

Mr. Stanley looked at his watch. "God, I didn't realize it was so late. May I take a rain check? I'd better get up to the hospital and then back to the office. We'll let you know if we find out anything on Mr. Pike's relatives."

"Okay, Berrien. Let's go eat."

Outside the reporters were still waiting, although there were less than earlier in the day. Etienne waved to them, and gave them the smile that resembled a wolfish grin. It was a frightening sight. Those of us who know him always scurry as far away from him as possible when he unleashes that particular facial expression. It means trouble for anyone unwise enough to bother him. The reporters didn't know that.

"Etienne, what's the latest? The FBI agent was here but he wouldn't talk to us. Tell us what's going on," said one young man while he pushed his foam-covered microphone close to 'Tienne's face.

"No comment."

"Oh, come on. We're working for a living."

"No. No comment."

"Look at all the free publicity you guys are getting."

Oops. That was definitely not the way to our hearts. What parent was going to be thrilled to send a child to us, no matter how good the facilities were, how wonderful the coaching was, with murders and kidnapping abounding?

Etienne lost his temper, as I knew he would as soon as I saw that phoney smile. He said a string of words in French. I knew they were not nice words but couldn't translate them exactly, nor did I try. The reporter's French was obviously better than mine. He turned a bright pink, the flush starting at his immaculate white shirt collar and moving upwards until even the tips of his ears glowed.

"'Tienne," I warned, "those microphones are live! You shouldn't use such language."

"I'll say what I want. Now. Are we going to lunch or not?"

We drove off in Etienne's immaculate 1990 Cadillac. Instead of the sunny day that had shown promise earlier, it was now seriously overcast, wind blowing all the way from Asia and picking up speed over every mile. A stand of feathery eucalyptus trees showered the highway with curling strips of bark. Snowy crested egrets erupted from the branches, dozens of them, tired of being blown about.

At the restaurant we managed a window table. I would have liked to sit outdoors so we could hear and smell the sea but it was now too cold and windy. In the few minutes it took to have our soup ordered and delivered the rain started. It was going to be a nasty storm. The water beat against the picture window. We couldn't see as far as the beach.

We ate in silence. Etienne was still in his black mood. I was tired and my throat threatened to cease working whenever it felt a morsel of solid food head its way. After what seemed like hours, we paid the check, bought a paper to put over our heads and ran for the car. We could have saved the paper money. The wind whipped the impromptu umbrellas in every direction but over our heads. Then, to make matters perfect

'Tienne dropped the car keys into the mud of the bedraggled flower bed by his side of the car.

After a silent ride back to the arena, we parted at the office door. I went on to get my skates on and go try to figure the choreography for the numbers I had taped in the morning. It always seemed as if time ran faster, the closer a show got, never enough time to get everything done—music, costumes, rehearsals, lighting, programs, all things that ate up time in big chunks.

The solos were blocked out, finally. Not the arms, of course. It was physically impossible while holding a clipboard in one hand and a portable tape deck in the other. As it was, there were numerous interruptions as I skated a section, went to the railing to write the sequence down and repeated the process again and yet again.

The kids were coming in from school. The rink was cold because of the heavy rain, still falling uninterrupted outside. The wind was wailing in frustration as it parted to go around the building only to rush together on the other side.

Marguerita came in with her dad, loaded down as usual, water dripping off her raincoat, hair soaking wet because her hat had blown off. Rodrigo, more experienced in such weather was drier inside a heavy parka with an attached hood. I went over and told 'Rita to come with me. There was a hair dryer in the pros' room and she could use that before she changed into a skating dress.

Rodrigo looked worried. I was sure he had more questions to ask about all the excitement surrounding the complex. I wasn't certain that those questions could be answered well enough to calm his anxieties. Certainly the sight of my throat wouldn't help so I carefully rearranged the soft scarf to hide the marks.

"Hi, Rodrigo. Miserable weather, isn't it? I'd better go find the dryer for Marguerita. I think we'll work on her back loops for about fifteen minutes and then really finish the *Malagueña* number today. Oh, is she going to be able to be here for the judges tomorrow? She doesn't have a test or anything in school, does she?"

"She'll be here," he said in his slow, deliberate voice. "You want her here at Noon, right?"

"That'll be great. She shouldn't have any trouble with it next week, but it's always helpful to get experience skating in front of judges."

"After her lesson, you will have a few minutes to talk to me about the problems here, won't you? Her mother is so worried."

"Of course," I replied and went off to get my student taken care of.

The next hour was fun. Working with the charming, serious Marguerita was always that and more. I had said fifteen minutes on the back loops and after the first two sets each of the outside edge and inside edge figures, I was ready to quit. They were ready for the test but Marguerita, like most elite skaters, was a perfectionist. She wanted to do more sets. Finally I had to say, "Stop! I'm getting dizzy—and you're the one doing the figures. Now, go change your skates and we'll work on freestyle."

"Okay, Berrien," she said and literally ran to get the freestyle skates on. "Did I tell you how much I like the show number? The music is wonderful. Mama loves it, too. She said she can hardly wait to see the show. She's going to come to the show! That'll be a first for her. You know, she's never come in here. Papa keeps asking her, too. He shows her the videotapes you give me but that's not the same thing, is it?"

"Rita, I'm so very glad your mother will come. It'll be great for you, and a load off your father's mind, too. Are your brothers and their families coming, too?"

"The whole family is going to be here. Different nights 'cause they have to arrange baby-sitting for all the little ones but they are coming."

We started to work on the footwork for *Malagueña*. Then head movements. Her dark eyes glowed, the smile irresistible. It was going to be a show-stopper. Then I had her skate the whole program through. The other kids stopped to watch it, giving Marguerita room so that she could put it all together without worrying about running into one of the other skaters.

During the second run-through, I saw Juliet and Brandi Taggert come in. Juliet's fur of the day was an unbelievable grey Persian lamb made to look like a German Army great coat. Tasteful as ever she was wearing black patent leather boots that disappeared under the curly fur. Well, at least she didn't have her usual backless sandals on. The weather was obviously horrendous outside. I had been enjoying teaching Marguerita so much that I had forgotten about the storm.

Brandi's forelock, er, bangs, were plastered to her forehead and straggling into her eyes. She had no coat at all on, just a glittery short, skating dress. It was done in fetching tones of sinful red and day-glo yellow, loaded down with every type of bead made—at least that's what it looked like from where I was standing. This was, no doubt, the designer costume for Brandi's Oriental solo. Water was dripping off the aurora crystal beads that decorated the bottom of every single petal of the multilayered skirt. She had her skates and guards on. This was obviously an entrance designed to stun the onlooker with its magnificence. It stunned, all right!

Behind her stood a giant, holding an umbrella with all of its ribs showing. The wind had torn the thing inside out. The man was huge, about six feet seven or eight and probably about two hundred and eighty pounds, maybe more. I guessed that the previous bodyguard hadn't been big enough. Since Deputy Sean Mather had just entered right behind the bedraggled trio I hoped to heaven that the muscleman wasn't carrying an unlicensed weapon.

"How do you like it? It's gorgeous, isn't it?" Juliet brayed. "It will make a star out of Brandi."

I opened my mouth to speak, then shut it. I wasn't certain of what I meant to say but was sure that it wasn't going to be anything remotely complementary. Then, turning to Brandi, "Don't you think you'd better get some dry practice clothes on? We need to polish off your solo. Have you been listening to the music?"

"Of course she has," her mother answered. "Brandi, run along and change your outfit. We don't want anything to happen to this one."

The hell we didn't!

Sean had gone into the office but I didn't have time to be nosy. Brandi's lesson loomed over my schedule and I remembered that Philip had said he would call at six o'clock sharp our time. I wanted to get home for that. I was weary, hungry and hurting and wanted the feeling of security and love he always managed to convey. I spoke to Rodrigo and told him I would talk to him tomorrow. He nodded gravely, aware of the undercurrents that just might explode before too long.

Brandi emerged from the dressing room clad in yet another new practice dress less obvious than the show costume but not by much. She handed me the music tape quickly and ran out onto the ice. I put the tape in the portable recorder to refresh my memory while Brandi warmed up.

I heard the familiar strains of her music and went through her program mentally while the music played. And played. And played with a different tune that wouldn't even remotely be categorized as Oriental music. Mrs. Taggert had added another three minutes to Brandi's solo.

No! No way! I barged into the office, the altered tape replaying the music. Mather was still with Etienne. I didn't care and went storming in to see them with no apologies. "I want you to listen to this…this abomination and then tell that woman where she can go!"

"Calm down, Berrien. What's the matter?"

"Just listen. You know the Oriental number. So listen. She has added onto Brandi's music. Who in blazes does she think she is? And did you see that costume Brandi had on when she came in? It looks like a chandelier designed for a house of ill repute. You have to talk to her now! I will not have this. I won't!" I screeched as I stamped my foot, then grabbed for the water pitcher. Screeching really wasn't what my throat needed at that exact moment.

The deputy was sitting with his mouth open, not believing that a supposedly grown woman could have a temper tantrum over a piece of music.

Etienne was listening to the music. He heard the sounds of T*he Yellow River Concerto* and then the added piece cut in. It had come off a Scottish bagpipe album. He stared at the tape player in disbelief. Then he smiled his evil smile.

"What we are going to do, Berrien, is leave this just like it is and go put it on the rink music system. Everyone will hear how horrible it is and neither you nor I will have to do a thing. The parents and kids will do it for us."

"No. That's mean, 'Tienne. Brandi will be humiliated. I want Juliet put in her place but I sure don't want that poor child hurt."

Etienne was not to be dissuaded. Once he had thought up a scheme, he rarely backed away from it. Good sense didn't enter in to it. He got up and went out to the sound system. I ran to Brandi and got her off the ice. I wasn't going to have her start her number and be made fun of.

The music was playing at an almost painful level. David, ever patient, got off the ice to come adjust the volume, unaware of what was happening. As the music moved into the bagpipe selection he winced and moved faster and with a clear purpose. When he saw Etienne standing at the tape deck he looked puzzled. Then he shouted, "Turn that thing down!"

"No, we're playing the whole tape."

After an eternity the music was over. Having been inexpertly cut on the count of one, the audience kept waiting to hear the ending. They had heard it. More people turned to look at us. One of the skating mothers, Mrs. Simeon of needle work fame, said, "What was that? I hope no one is going to have to skate to that piece. It was awful."

Juliet came out of her seat. "What do you mean awful? Brandi is going to skate to it. That's all her solo. I picked the last part out last night at home. So stirring."

The woman was unbelievable. The only answer to the music question had to be that she was completely tone deaf. The costume was pure "B" Hollywood, of course.

'Tienne called to her, "Mrs. Taggert, I need to talk to you, please. Do you have a minute?"

"Of course. Now?"

"Yes, now."

Juliet went into the office and I told Brandi to go skate and I'd get her another tape. "Don't worry, Brandi. Etienne will get everything settled. And we'll keep the new tape here."

The bodyguard was looking from me to the office door as if he wasn't sure whether he was needed for Mrs. Taggert or should he stay within sight of his young charge. Deciding to stay by Brandi, he settled his bulk onto one of the benches.

Juliet was still in Etienne's office when I got off the ice and made my way to the pros' room. I hoped she was going to be there when I left the rink, too. One more word out of her and I wouldn't be responsible for my actions.

Gillian saw me go past her window and let Misty Joy out. We wove our way past still hopeful media types and were soon on our way home.

Chapter 13

Ah, home! No reporters, no Mrs. Juliet Taggert. I glanced at the clock. It was quarter til six, plenty of time before Philip called. We went into the kitchen and I fed the pooch. She hated it when Philip was on a trip because I rarely cooked a meal so there were precious few table goodies for her. I took a small container of home-made chili out of the freezer and popped it in the microwave. It was certainly chili weather. The rain lashed at the sliding doors even harder than it had at lunchtime at the restaurant. I chopped some fresh onion and grated some cheese for topping. A salad would normally be added to the menu but I didn't think chunks of lettuce would make it down my still aching throat.

I curled up on the couch, close to the phone. I could have used the portable but somehow I could never have enough confidence in something that wasn't apparently connected to anything else for these across-the-world calls. I was always afraid that we would be disconnected or the battery would run down.

Precisely at six the phone rang and I picked it up. "Hi, darling," I cooed.

"I didn't know you cared," said a perfectly strange male voice.

"Who are you?"

"Obviously, I'm darling."

"Look, I'm expecting a call from my husband. I'll have to hang up now. Whatever you're selling, I'm not buying," I said and slammed the phone down. My ears were as red as the young reporter's had been earlier in the day. I barely got my hands off the phone before it rang again. "Hello," I said cautiously.

"That's an innovative greeting for your husband. I expected something a little more enthusiastic."

"Oh, honey. I'm glad it's you but the excitement was used up on the call that came right at six. I called a total stranger 'darling.' Then hung up on him when I discovered it wasn't you."

He laughed. "How's everything going? Do you all know who killed the twins' uncle? And what about the case of the disappearing skater? Has she been located yet? Tell me all the news."

We had a long talk then about the mysterious events that seemed to be plaguing *N'ice Skates*. All, that is, except my nearly being throttled. I didn't think that he needed to hear about that incident while he was so far away. On second thought, it might be better if he heard it at a distance. He would have calmed down by the time he got home and wouldn't pose a threat to Pike's well-being, so we finally talked about it.

"I've been wondering why your voice sounded so strained and husky," said Philip. "I thought maybe you were just coming down with a cold, or something. It's a good thing you told me now. I would have hated to find out when I got home. Are you really okay?"

"Oh, sure. Sore and bruised but no permanent damage. Pike really got the worst of it with broken fingers and a heart attack."

Philip chuckled. "Little Sheli breaking his fingers. That's funny in a sick sort of way. And he taught her how to do it. Why, I wonder?"

"Oh, you know. Tension breaker—excuse the expression—at a competition sometime, probably. Ask her sometime. But I wouldn't ask for a demonstration if I were you."

We had talked for over half an hour. I was feeling loved and cared for once again. We said our goodbys. I was really looking forward to his homecoming now. There was still a lot of snow in the mountains. Maybe we could go skiing for a couple of days when he got back.

The microwave had beeped ages ago. I scooped up the onion bits and the shredded cheese and dumped them on top of the chili and heated everything up again. Misty was watching hopefully. She loved chili.

I took the hot food, a bottle of beer and the portable phone and sat down on a stool at the breakfast bar. Misty kept her eyes on the bowl as I ate the highly spiced food small spoonful by smaller spoonful. Not too painful so I kept on going. The cold beer helped to wash it down and I saved a little bit of the chili for my furry companion.

The phone rang again. I got it on the first ring. It was Etienne.
"Now what??"
"Berrien, can I come over? I've got to talk to someone and I don't want to do it on the telephone. Are you on that damn portable?"
"Yes, why?"
"Don't you know that anyone with a scanner can listen in? With all the reporters around you shouldn't be using that thing. Did Philip call?"
"Yes, just when he said he would. Why?"
"I hope you weren't on the portable then if you talked about all our problems."
"I didn't use it, so don't worry."
"Well, can I come on over? I just learned something that I need to tell someone."
"Sure. Come on. Have you had dinner? I'll fix you something if you haven't. But 'Tienne, if you learned anything shouldn't you be talking to Mather or the FBI? I can't do anything."
"No. What I learned, I heard from them. It's not...oh, damn it. I'm on my way. See you in about twenty minutes."

I sat back on the sofa, wondering what had Etienne so upset. Generally, he was pretty unflappable. He had been tossed out of his home at the tender age of fifteen and had been on his own since then. It hadn't been an easy life although he never complained. Just told his funny stories about scrapes he had gotten into and how he got out of them.

His marriages, disasters though they had been, were always resolved amicably and he is still friendly with all three ladies. In fact, he is godfather to two of the ladies' children. And he never says a nasty word about any of them.

It must be something really serious to have him so very upset. Well, he'd be at the house shortly, then I'd find out what the problem was.

The phone rang again. I jumped, then picked it up.

"Am I calling too late? We just saw Mr. Stanley of the FBI. He gave us your kind invitation."

Invitation? What invitation? "Oh, Mrs. Tompson. I'm glad he remembered. We have plenty of room here. I just thought it might help you while we're all waiting for a resolution to both the crimes if you were to be around Tami's friends. When would you like to come down?"

"If you're sure it's all right, we'll come down tomorrow."

"Of course it's all right. Do you want me to come up and pick you up?"

"No. We've rented a car. We'll go to the rink. Mr. Stanley said we'd have a hard time finding your house. Is that good?"

"That sounds fine. Okay, I'll see you tomorrow. And I'll tell Paul you're going to be here. It'll cheer him up, I hope."

After the call I made some fresh coffee and got the remains of an angel food cake out of the freezer, along with some strawberries. Etienne always wanted sweets so I whirled the strawberries, some milk and confectioner's sugar in the blender, ready to pour over the cake.

Misty ran to the front door, tail wagging, long before 'Tienne was even out of his car. By the time I let him in, she was wriggling around on her back so that one of her favorite "uncles" could scratch her tummy.

"Berrien. This is awful! Terrible!" he began before he even got his jacket off.

"Come on to the family room. I've got a fire going. Give me your jacket. I'll throw it in the dryer. You look like you walked all the way here instead of driving." The rain was still coming down as if poured continuously from heavenly buckets. "Sit down. Want some coffee? I've got cake, too."

"No coffee. Scotch. In a big glass."

"Etienne, you have to drive back. That road isn't in good condition in bright sunlight, never mind tonight in the rain."

"Scotch. Now. Please."

I sighed but knew that in his current mood he wouldn't give up. He'd have to stay overnight. I got a double on-the-rocks glass out and poured a small amount of scotch in it and added loads of ice. He took it, drank the liquor and went over to the sink and dumped the ice out. Then grabbed the bottle and filled the glass again, without any ice. Satisfied that he was supplied for awhile, he sat down. Misty jumped up to join him and sprawled over his lap.

"Now, what is terrible, horrible and all those other adjectives or adverbs or whatever you were using?"

"Pike."

"Well, he certainly hasn't been in the running for the Mr. Congeniality prize this week but so bad? Is he worse? Dead? What?"

"He's very sick."

"Etienne, of course he's sick. He's just had a heart attack, open heart surgery, a young woman broke a couple of his fingers and he was bitten by a dog. He's apparently been like a disturbed hibernating bear for over a year so something has been bugging him. And you say he's sick!"

"No, not the heart trouble. I've just talked to his surgeon. He wanted information on his relatives. The manager of his arena called me back a little while ago. No one at the rink knew of any relatives—not even any close friends. I talked to Paul. He said that Pike never invited any of the skaters to his house. Not even when he did their music. He was always polite, at least up until last year but was obsessively private. Paul doesn't even know where he came from. The manager said he'd check on his résumé tomorrow if his secretary can find it. You know he's been at that rink for donkey's years. The police there are asking for a warrant to get into the house. They hope maybe they'll find some personal information there. If a judge gives them permission to go in we may learn more about the man."

"There wasn't anything in his wallet as who to notify?"

"No. Doctor Givens is concerned. There are...well, complications with his condition."

"Stop procrastinating, Etienne. Come out with what you are trying to say."

"He has AIDS. Full blown. Mather finally found out where he had been staying. A hotel over at SFO. His suitcase held a few clothes and a whole lot of medicine for AIDS. And, of course, he didn't get any of that medication today. The deputy brought it over to the hospital so the doctors are trying to get in contact with the doctor who prescribed the stuff. So far no luck. Doctor Givens is getting a specialist down from the city to try to sort out what all the pills are. He needs to know so he doesn't give Pike medicine that he shouldn't give him."

"Can Pike talk yet?"

"Givens said that he can be interviewed shortly by Mather tomorrow. Sean thinks that he is mixed up in our recent difficulties but doesn't know how. He needs to question him."

"What do the FBI people think? Has Sean talked to them? It seems so...so improbable. More like a soap opera."

'Tienne had been taking large gulps of scotch from the glass. It was already well below the half-way mark.

"Have you eaten?"

"Not since lunch. And now I'm not hungry. That disease. We have lost so many friends. I'm really frightened for Tami. If Pike is really responsible for her kidnapping, what happens if he won't tell us where she is? He won't be out of the hospital for days. She could starve to death. Berrien, it's a nightmare!"

He was right, of course. On both counts. "But 'Tienne, Tami was shown with this morning's paper on a video tape delivered early this morning. Pike went to the hospital last night. He couldn't have made the video himself. Somebody else knows where she is, and must be taking care of her. Maybe we need to hold a press conference. Tell everyone that Vaughan will be out of commission for days. I bet that's what was meant by that 'unavoidable delay' comment in Tami's message."

The scotch glass was empty. Etienne was contemplating it appraisingly. His movements were hindered by the big white dog happily ensconced on his lap, snoring again. I heaved a sigh and got up and refilled it for him. Before I handed it to him I held out my hand. "Car keys, please."

"No, I'll be okay to drive."

"No keys, no scotch."

"They're in my coat pocket."

"No they're not. Your jacket is still in the dryer and they weren't in it. Give. Misty, move over so 'Tienne can get his keys out." Her long, white eyelashes flickered open. She got down off the couch and went over to the door. Time to go out. He dug in his trouser pocket and handed me the whole jangly bunch that he normally carried around with him. I handed him the glass.

I was restless and paced the family room floor as we continued to talk. Remembering the uninvited stranger who had been outside the house several nights ago, I turned on the outside lights again and let the dog in. I dried her off with her very own ivory-colored beach towel. She lay down in front of the fire to finish the drying in time-honored doggy fashion.

"'Tienne, did you talk to Doctor Givens about Pike's illness?"

"No. He wouldn't talk about it. I'm not a relative or anything. But he asked if Pike had injured his ankle and cut his chin during the fracas at the store."

The room was filled with the smell of wet dog. The fire crackled as a log broke and dropped down to the bottom. Wind and water were hurling themselves at the windows and doors.

We sat silent, listening to the violence of the weather outside. What a lonely man Pike seemed to be. Even though the people at his arena knew he was seriously ill, not one of his students or their parents had called the hospital. At least that's what Mather had told Etienne.

I was aware of a deep gratitude for my family, scattered though we usually were. Etienne knew that he too had family. Not blood-related but from years of friendship.

"I wonder if Pike was my mysterious visitor the other night? He could have gotten injuries like that from the deck. What about Uncle Tomaso? Are they any closer to finding out who killed him or why he had come back to this area?"

"Mather is certain that Tami's kidnapping is mixed up with the old man's death but there's no one to ask about why he came back here. Maybe he just wanted to come home. The coroner said that he didn't have long to live in any case. A bad heart and a bad liver."

"How's Mrs. Andrade doing? She hasn't been in the rink the last day or so. At least, I haven't seen her."

"She's fine. After all, she and Tomaso weren't close. He was a lot older than she is and she hadn't seen him in years. The rest of her sisters and brothers are all gone, too. She's the baby of the family. She'll have the funeral next week and then go back up to Sea Ranch. I hope."

"She's not the most soothing person to be around, is she? I remember her at competitions when Miki and Sheli were competing. She was a terror. Even the year they were Pike's team. I thought she was going to brain him with her handbag—suitcase would be a better word for it—over something he had said to the kids. That was before they won Nationals. It's a wonder another pro would take them on. Maybe that's why Pike's so obsessed with Tami and Paul. Think so?"

"It probably has something to do with it. But if he's really sick maybe he knows that he won't have another chance to have a national pair championship team."

Etienne's glass was empty again but he was slouching down on the sofa. His big, brown eyes were blinking slowly. He would soon be asleep. I knew I had better get him into bed soon or he would be sleeping on the couch all night.

I went into the closest guest room and turned the covers down. "Come on 'Tienne. Bed time."

He unfolded himself from the couch. "*Oui*. I guess you're right, Berrien. Which room?"

"I put the light on and the bed's turned down. There's a toothbrush in the bathroom for you and a fresh razor for in the morning. I'll see you then."

He ambled into the hallway. I followed to make sure he got to the right room. He did. Took off his shoes and got under the covers and fell asleep instantly.

I went back to the family room to tidy up. Misty was still snoozing in front of the fire, totally dry now. She woke up, went over to the door but decided she didn't need another bath.

We padded down to the bedroom. Again, she got up on the bed even without my invitation. I crawled in, close to her, needing companionship. What a rotten world. I lay, wide awake in the dark. The storm outside suited my mood well.

I thought back. Over thirty years ago, the United States skating community had lost over fifty fine skaters, judges, coaches, parents and friends in a still unexplained plane crash outside of Brussels. Out of that terrible tragedy had come some good. The United States Figure Skating Association Memorial Fund had been set up to honor the skaters. Even now it provides funds for talented young skaters to continue their careers in a sport that can become horrendously expensive.

Over the past ten years, we had been losing friends, acquaintances and rivals one at a time to the insidious AIDS. I decided the former was less traumatic than the current situation. Poor Vaughan Pike.

After a long while, I fell into a restless sleep.

CHAPTER 14

The smell of bacon sizzling was wending its way down the hallway. My faithful dog had deserted me. I remembered that we had a guest, got up quickly and hurried into the kitchen. Misty had her head on Etienne's foot. He was standing at the stove, tending the frying pan. Alongside, on the counter was a bowl with the makings for one of his special omelets. Onions, green peppers, and tomatoes were all chopped up ready to go into the mixture.

"Morning, Berrien. I though we needed a decent meal to start off today. It'll be busy with the judges coming over and we probably won't get lunch. Just sit down. I'll serve the food when it's ready. Some coffee?"

"Oh, yes, thanks." It had been a long time since anyone had fixed me breakfast. Philip has many good points but cooking isn't numbered among his skills.

We sat and ate quietly, talking mostly about the day's mock judging and how the show was coming along. We had the ballet rehearsal later in the evening. Ariadne had promised to be there to help put it together. I was looking forward to working with her.

Etienne finished eating and cleaned up the kitchen. Then he said, "May I have my keys now, please? And thank you for listening to me and taking the keys last night. I wouldn't have made it home. Oh, where's my jacket?"

"Still in the dryer, probably all wrinkled! I'll go get it." I was right. It looked like an aged prune.

"Never mind. It's warm out now. I'll just take it to the cleaner's later."

He was right. Yesterday's storm had moved inland and the wooden deck was glistening in the sunlight. No sand sullied its' smooth surface. Far out to sea were two freighters headed north into San Francisco Bay. White clouds, looking scrubbed and ready for church, skittered across the sky.

I soon followed Etienne to the rink. I didn't even have a scarf wrapped around my neck. The bruises were fading. Now it just looked like I hadn't washed my neck recently. A couple of TV vans were back at, or still at, I wasn't sure which, the parking lot. There must have been newer mayhem for the multitudes to scurry after.

Gillian was in the office on the phone again. The poor lady had done nothing all week but answer the telephones or make calls. I bet she was looking forward to the weekend. We kept the office staffed on the weekends by junior college students who were taking business management courses. We got good help that way and they had a chance to earn some money while getting practical business experience. We were all winners.

She called me to come in. 'Tienne was on the phone in his office. He still needed to go change his clothes and shave. He had obviously been on his way when the call came in. He wasn't his usual casually elegant self. He gestured to me to come on in. "It's the manager at Pike's arena," he whispered.

"Yes, I understand. But the doctors won't let any of us see him or talk to him. You can't find any sign of any kin? How about a lawyer? Does he have an attorney?"

He put the phone on the speaker phone again so I could hear the other side of the conversation.

"We can't find any sign of relatives," replied the manager.

"Are there any of the skaters' parents who are lawyers? Particularly one of Pike's kids? That would be a logical choice for him to make," I asked. "Can you try that route? It's become critical that the hospital gets this information."

"Why? Is he worse? Is he dead?"

"Not that we know of," Etienne reassured him. "It's just that the doctors need some background information and to know where he will be going to recuperate. He's mostly sleeping now, but he still can't talk because of all the tubes and such."

"Well, I'll check with the parents. See what I can find out about a lawyer and call you back," said the manager.

There was a commotion out by the ice surface and we both jumped up to look. A strange man and woman were hugging Paul. The lady was crying, the man doing the macho male act of strong and silent. Etienne and I went out to meet them.

Paul made the introductions, "Etienne, Berrien, these are Tami's parents."

"'ow do you do?" asked Etienne with his best fractured English act. "It is a pleasure to finally meet you. Although I am so *distrait* about the circumstances."

"I'm glad you could come. It must have been terribly lonely waiting for news in a hotel room. Come, have some coffee," I invited.

All five of us moved into 'Tienne's office where he was dispensing fresh coffee and doughnuts that he had gotten from a bakery on his way back to the arena. They were for the pros meeting which I had forgotten about. Well, it was going to be very short because of the visiting judges anyhow, so the pros wouldn't need food.

Mrs. Tompson was tiny, round and grey haired. She had the peaches and cream complexion that is usually associated with English ladies. When she spoke we realized that she was, indeed, from England originally. She wore a Laura Ashley print dress, low-heeled pumps and a sweater of cornflower blue that picked up the blue in the print and matched her eyes.

Her husband was tall, almost as tall as Paul, and slender. He was casually dressed in slacks, polo shirt and tweedy jacket with highly polished black loafers. It was difficult to determine his hair color because he was almost completely bald and what there was of it was clipped extremely short.

They sank into the comfortable chairs and sipped some coffee. Neither were interested in doughnuts. There was an uncomfortable silence, none of us knowing what to say.

"It is extremely kind of you to ask us to visit," said Mrs. Tompson. "You are right in saying that the hotel room was lonely. We haven't ever been to San Francisco before but we were afraid to leave the hotel. We wanted to be where we would get any news right away."

"I wish I had thought of it sooner. You did tell the FBI you were coming down, didn't you? If not we'll call them right now."

"Oh, yes," Mr. Tompson said. He had a wonderful baritone voice, reminding me of the actor, Claude Akins. "Mr. Stanley thought it was a good idea. That way, when they have any information they can get us all at once."

"Would you like to go out to the house now or would you like to stay here for awhile? We're having trial judging in a little while for some of the lower tests. And tonight I'm afraid we have a show rehearsal but it's only for two hours. You might like to watch that. Paul could take you out to the house if you'd like to rest for awhile."

"Oh, we'd rather stay here. Around people. It will give us something to do."

Etienne called to Gillian. "Come in and meet Tami's parents. They'll be staying with Berrien for awhile."

Our much-put-upon secretary came into 'Tienne's office, followed by Misty Joy who knew that there would be no candy if Gillian wasn't there. They were both introduced to the Tompsons.

The first of the judges had arrived, Marlene Oligivy. She was a high test judge, a former skater herself and on her way to becoming a World Judge. As with all judges in the sport, Marlene loved skating, understood its pressures and cared about the young kids involved in the sport. We were lucky to have her with us.

A few minutes later, an apparently crotchety old man came in, holding the furriest boots I had ever seen, one in each hand. He was a legendary judge, had been an International Judge for many years but had recently retired after spending fifty years crawling around the ice. Mr. Harold Raines had seen every skater of note in his long career.

We were fortunate to have these two people. The best of the old guard and the finest of the new, younger people coming up the ranks. It would be an interesting session for all of us.

Mr. Raines would often tell funny stories about competitions of long-ago days. One of his favorites had to do with a World Championship in Colorado Springs in 1957.

An American skater was skating the last of the six required figures. With one minor flaw in the six tracings, the back paragraph three looked as if it had been skated only once. It would be difficult to do a figure that perfect on a piece of paper using pencil and compass. By the time Tim had skated the last tracing, no one in the arena was breathing. As he skated off a great whoosh of breath could be heard from a red-faced audience.

The judges, clustered around the figure, clipboards in hand, ready to note any flaws, slipped and slid around the two circles. One judge, from Hungary or Romania, was intent on finding errors. He was of more than ample rotundity and was dressed in an almost full length beaver coat with a beaver hat pulled down over his ears. At last, unable to find anything wrong while walking around, he literally lay down on the ice and paddled around the figure, looking for all the world like a beached walrus.

What a pity home video cameras weren't available in those days. A priceless picture!

Everyone began to gather rinkside. The students who were taking part in the mock tests were dressed and ready. We sent them out onto the ice which Etienne had just finished. It looked so slippery I was worried about Mr. Raines going out on it.

Miki, Sheli, Etienne, David and I gathered at the railings giving last minute instructions to the students. The kids knew it was a practice session. We were acting as if it were the last round of the Olympics.

Brandi and Marguerita were out working on the figures they were going to skate. Rodrigo had settled down in his customary seat in the bleachers with his back supported by a column. Mrs. Taggert and the bodyguard sat near him, she for once blessedly silent. Other parents sat scattered around or in the snack shop which had the advantage of being walled-off with plexiglass from the ice surfaces and therefore was marginally warmer.

After the review session, we had lunch in the snack bar, students, pros, parents and the visiting judges. We all agreed that it had been a productive time. Both Marlene and Mr. Raines were pleased with the arena. Neither one had ever seen it before. Mr. Raines, originally from the mid-west had retired to Pacific Grove several years ago and he volunteered to be available for more sessions as we needed him.

"After all, it's not a long drive and I love to ride along the ocean. It's a never ending pleasure. I'm sure my wife would like to come, too."

We waved goodby to the two judges and returned to the rink. Etienne was called back into the office for another phone call. Just as we were walking in, Trick arrived.

"It's a surprise to see you here today, Trick. Aren't you supposed to be here on Saturdays?" David asked.

"I guess I'm just wound up. With everything that's going on, you know? I'll go up and do some workouts for awhile." He left and tromped up the stairs.

"Who was that?" Mrs. Tompson asked. "He looks sort of familiar."

"Our weight trainer. His name's Trick Brewster," David said. "Where do you think you've seen him?"

"I thought maybe....No, I'm imagining things. We've been so upset. It's just that he looks somewhat like that young man that hung around the arena where Paul and Tami skated, you know, with Vaughan Pike."

David turned to Paul, "Does he look familiar to you?"

"No, but I wasn't there as long as Tami was. When was this man at that rink, Mrs. Tompson?"

"Oh, several years ago. Before you started skating with Tami, I'm sure. Let's forget it. I'm sure I'm mistaken. That certainly was interesting to see the children working with the judges. We never had anything like it at the rinks where Tami skated."

By this time, more children were arriving to skate public session before the rehearsal. The shouting, running and general horseplay finally settled down as everyone got their skates on and went out on the ice to use up excess energy in a useful fashion.

Ariadne floated in, dressed in warm slacks, a hand-knit sweater that had to be from Norway, and sneakers. She was carrying a skate bag. As I watched with my mouth open she put on a pair of well-used custom skates.

"What are you going to do?" I asked her.

"I want to try some of the arm movements I'm thinking of before we try to teach them to the skaters. Some of them might not work on the ice."

"I didn't know you could skate."

"Oh, not really well. We weren't encouraged to do things other than ballet, you know. But I really loved skating so I learned a little bit. Actually, I learned mostly ice-dancing and a few spins. I didn't do very many jumps, though."

"What a bonus you are! And I bet you'll impress all the parents, too. Do you need my portable tape deck?"

"No, I've got one here," she said as she patted her pocket and put a headset on. "The music's wonderful. All Strauss waltzes. The number will just float."

She was so enthusiastic about it, I didn't want to tell her that the kids of today were totally unable to count music that was anything other than four beats per bar. That small problem had all ready made for some interesting collisions during earlier rehearsals. To add arm movements now was really going to be fun—or funny.

Sean Mather had returned and was again talking to Etienne. They saw me and motioned for me to come in.

"Hi. I can only stay a minute. I ought to get the Tompsons to my place before the practice starts. They could probably use some rest."

"No, they've already said that they want to stay and watch. Then we're all going out to dinner. Sean here has some more information that's very interesting."

"Oh, what's that?"

"He's turned up someone with an arrest record. Oh, I'll let him tell it."

"Who?"

"It's a man by the name of Richard Wellington. You remember all those finger prints we took when we were here on Monday?"

"Sure. We still don't have all that stuff cleaned away. It floated all over the place."

"Well, we found a lot of this guy's prints around here. In the office, on doors, in the men's room, upstairs in the weight room, in the dance studio. He was arrested and served two years for armed robbery. He only got two years because he was only eighteen at the time and he didn't have any previous record."

"When was he released?"

"About eight years ago. He finished his two years probation and disappeared from his home town. Both parents are dead. Mother died last year, father's been dead for about five years."

"I sure haven't met anyone with that name, have you, Etienne?"

"No. But it could be almost anyone. We're open to the public. And we have loads of workmen in to fix plumbing and electricity or to do painting. There have even been caterers in to serve food for some of the birthday parties. I don't see how this helps anything, Sean."

"I don't either but at least it's something to look into. The prints don't match any of yours, anyhow. Oh, yes, this guy's prints were on the sherry bottle, too as well as Uncle Tomaso's. Well, I just wanted to let you all know the latest. See you."

"Bye for now," I said.

Etienne went out to make the ice before the rehearsal and I joined Ariadne. "Did you get everything worked out? No, of course not, you don't know the positions of the girls. I should have remembered that and come out with you. I'm sorry. We'll just have to work on it now. We'll have them skate the whole number for you first."

"That'll work fine."

The Zamboni ceased its clatter and we got out onto the ice.

"Ladies, this is Ariadne. Some of you already know her. She's the ballet teacher and has volunteered to help us make this number truly lovely. I want you all in the beginning positions and then to skate the entire number. No stopping until the music is over."

Thirty-six girls, tall and short, scooted onto the ice, did the inevitable little jumps and spins and finally took their opening positions for the number. I went to the sound system and started the music.

It had been two weeks since this number had been practiced. It looked it. The girls were all over the place, one circle, supposed to start with turns to the right, managed it fine. A second circle of twelve was definitely confused. Several, watching the front group, went to the right while the rest, remembering the choreography correctly started to the left, but off-beat.

I let them muddle on. The movements would at least give Ariadne an idea of the number and its supposed directions. Furthermore, if I stopped it now I would yell a lot and my throat wasn't ready for loud noises coming from it. Etienne was standing by the Zamboni room door, watching. It was only going to be a short time before he got his skates on and dove into the fray, too.

The phone was ringing. Gillian had left for the day, and a peaceful weekend. 'Tienne hurried to catch it at the skate counter. He spoke for a minute and then moved into the office after putting the line on hold.

Strauss' waltz music filled the arena. I defy anyone to keep their feet and bodies still while listening to the lilting melodies of old Vienna. The parents of the skaters were swaying from side to side, feet tapping in time to the music. For the next hour Ariadne and I worked with the girls. We broke the music into sections and skated the number the way we wanted it.

The twelve smaller girls would be wearing the short tutus and the twenty-four taller girls were going to have the longer dresses, all in a bright, true green that would look lovely under the spotlights. The four soloists were also wearing green but lighter shades than the *corps de ballet*. If we could get everyone to remember the program it would be stunning. That "if" was going to give me an ulcer over the next month or so.

Friday night public sessions were usually crowded. The people were coming in early to watch the rehearsal. We had never allowed people to watch practices at other rinks. Here, we thought it was a good idea. The people of Portugal could see how hard the skaters worked and would be sure to come to one of the actual performances to see the finished product. At this disastrous point in time we needed all the good will we could get.

I had seen Trick come down and go into the front office. Etienne was still on the phone in his private lair. I wondered who he had been speaking to for so long.

Finally we finished the rehearsal with another complete run through of the entire number including the solos. Everyone went in the proper direction at the planned time, no one bumped into someone else and the impromptu audience clapped wildly. If that was the reception of the program on practice ice with no spotlights and no fancy costumes, the thing was bound to be a hit in the show. At least I hoped so.

Ariadne and I thanked the girls and got off the ice. Both of us were exhausted. It had been a long week and we still had the Saturday morning classes to do tomorrow.

She took her skates off and was putting them into her skate bag.

"Ariadne, do you want to keep your skates here? You can have a locker in the pros' room if you like. Then you wouldn't have to cart them around."

"Oh, I have a locker upstairs in the dance room. Why don't I just keep them there? I never even thought of that. What a good idea. I'm just used to always hauling them around."

"Do you want to come have dinner with us? Mr. and Mrs. Tompson, Etienne, David and I are all going. You're welcome to come with us."

"That sounds like fun. Terry is out of town so I don't have to hurry home. Thank you."

We went into the pros' room to tidy up. Life on the Coast is casual, even on a Friday night but not quite as causal as we were after our hour and a half on the ice with forty young ladies. Hair combed, make-up reapplied, we headed to the office.

Trick Brewster was sitting in Gillian's chair, looking stunned. Since he hadn't been overly concerned about any of the happenings over the past eventful week, I wondered what had caused this about face.

"Are you okay?" I asked, "you look upset about something."

"Huh? Oh, yeah, yeah. I'm okay. Guess I'm just tired. I worked out a lot this afternoon."

While I couldn't warm up to this young man, I felt that we should invite him along to dinner. "We're all going out to dinner now. Would you like to join us?"

"Huh? Oh, no, thank you. I'd better be getting home. It's a long drive to San Francisco and my car is still acting up. I'll see you tomorrow. 'Night." He got up and wandered outside.

"Well, I wonder what hit him? Oh, well, I guess we're all acting a little strangely this week." I poked my head around the door frame. David and Etienne were talking quietly. "You guys ready for dinner? Ariadne's coming with us."

"Good. You two were really working out there. That number's going to be great. That is, if the girls remember it," David said.

There was that "if" again.

"When are we going to start the Russian number? Not next Tuesday, I hope."

"No, I scheduled it for the following Tuesday and Friday. Maybe if we do two sessions the same week everyone will remember it. We're doing the Oriental program on Tuesday and then I think Friday I'll do both the junior and senior octets. Tomorrow, between the classes and public session I have the Tiny Tot number scheduled. You know—*The Wizard of Oz* number."

"Let's go. I'm starving," Etienne grumbled.

Paul, who had eaten earlier declined an invitation to come with us and volunteered to take care of Misty Joy. In fact, he said he'd walk her home. I gave him a key to the house and feeding instructions for her.

We headed for the *Boat Dock*. Etienne had called for reservations. Not necessary during the week but on weekends we get a lot of visitors from the Peninsula side and seating at a favorite eatery can be non-existent.

Chapter *15*

We were on time and got the big table in the corner where we could all watch the activity in the harbor. The windows were open to a glorious evening, a real change from the previous night.

I glanced nervously around. Pike's attack had made me jumpy even though I was surrounded by friends and I knew he was still in intensive care. There were several reporters enjoying the restaurant's fabulous food but they at least pretended to ignore us.

Mr. and Mrs. Tompson were naturally very quiet. Worry had etched new lines on both their faces. Tami was an only child and they hadn't had her until Mrs. Tompson was forty.

Etienne was looking very thoughtful and, unusual for him, indecisive. He spoke up, having made up his mind to tell us about the phone conversation he had had with Doctor Givens, Pike's surgeon. He looked over cautiously at the reporters at their table. They were having a good time and the wine was flowing rapidly from bottles to glasses to throats.

"Doctor Givens called me a little while ago. He wanted to check again to see if we had located any relatives for Mr. Pike. The doctor is in a quandary. He doesn't know what to do. He told me that his patient has been babbling about a murder but that he hasn't been specific. The doctor's worried that Pike may be talking about Uncle Tomaso—what is his last name, anyhow?"

I glanced at the Tompsons. "The doctor was specific? A murder. Not plural?"

"Yes. Givens said that Pike was saying things like 'It shouldn't have happened. I told him to be careful.'"

"Who is 'him'?"

"The doctor didn't know."

"Don't you think we had better tell Mather? You didn't promise him not to talk to anyone, did you?"

"Even if I had, which I didn't, I would still tell the police but Doctor Givens said he would call them. He thinks that Pike will be strong enough to answer questions by tomorrow. At least he'll be off the strong pain killers, enough to make sense and understand what the cops are asking him. The FBI needs to talk to him, too, remember."

"That's good news. He must know something about Tami's disappearance. Otherwise, why would he be around here instead of teaching at his rink? Did Givens say anything more about Pike's other problem?"

David, the Tompsons and Ariadne looked at me in surprise.

"What other problem?" David asked.

"I really shouldn't say anything more," Etienne weaseled. "I only talked to Berrien last night because I was so upset."

"Pike has AIDS." Ariadne stated it as a simple fact, not as a question. Her world of ballet was as much a victim of the disease as our skating fraternity was.

"Yes. The deputy found the medication in his motel room yesterday. He told Doctor Givens and delivered the medicine to him. Givens did talk to Pike's doctors today," Etienne recalled, talking in a very low voice, aware that the journalists were still at a near-by table. "That's one of the reasons that Givens called me, why it is so imperative that his relatives are located. Pike's doctors told Givens that he is slowly losing his mind. He has all sorts of delusions. He no longer can reason at all. It has a fancy name but what it amounts to is a type of dementia. None of the medications help with that. That's why he has been acting so oddly over the past year."

Mrs. Tompson spoke up. "Tami said that he was changing so much. She hardly realized it was the same coach she had known for so long. She couldn't understand it."

"He was cussing out judges at Nationals, too. He never did that before," David said. "It was almost as if he knew he wouldn't be at another competition. And then he had to take Tami and Paul to World's. I bet he felt like a fool. Mrs. Tompson, did he behave himself properly at World's?"

"Oh, no. He yelled at a German judge and at the American one. He called them all sorts of names. I thought we were at a baseball game and the players were arguing with the umpires! His language was appalling. And in front of all those young people. He was sort of staggering, too, like he'd had too much to drink. But now that I think of it, I've never seen him take a drink of alcohol."

"I haven't either," put in Mr. Tompson. "He's been to meals and parties at our house for years. He never even drank wine. He always said it would set a bad example for his students."

The reporters were all leaving. I hoped they had a designated driver or the accident would tie up traffic for hours.

The waiters were busy filling every inch of our table with food. The *Boat Dock* was famous on the Coast—and a favorite with everyone from the rink. We always got great service because we would bring internationally known coaches and skaters here whenever they came to visit the arena complex.

They served only one kind of salad at any given meal and when there were more than four people in a party the customers got a big bowl of it to serve among themselves. They had learned that we all loved to eat but were always weight conscious so we got a huge bowl of the salad for the six of us. The plates of fish, salmon, Ahi tuna and rainbow trout, were put in front of us, along with my own favorite cioppino, which Ariadne had also ordered.

Conversation stopped while we tasted the food. We had only had tea sandwiches for lunch and were all hungry. Even Mr. and Mrs. Tompson ate heartily. It was doing them good to be with people who were sharing their worry over Tami.

After dinner we went back to the rink and straightened ourselves out carwise. The Tompsons were going to follow me home and Etienne went into the rink to check on any problems. David and Ariadne got into their respective cars and drove off home.

The Tompsons, by now sorted into Dan and Beverly, drove carefully, slowly, behind me. I signaled the turn into our lane and they followed, more cautiously. Paul had left the porch light on and one in the family room. I could see them as we pulled up to the house.

Misty Joy got to her paws slowly. She was not pleased to have been brought home and unceremoniously left alone, even if she had been walked along her favorite path and handsomely fed. However, when she saw that I wasn't alone she perked up. In her opinion she is the center of the universe and the more admirers the better.

Dan brought the luggage in and I led them to Trent's bedroom. I had not had a chance to strip and remake the guest room bed.

"Sorry about the 'young male' decor. This is my son's room and I haven't gotten around to making it looking more adult. He's graduating from med school in June. It's hard to believe. I don't feel old enough, myself."

"Tami's room is still all over girlish. You know, all pink and ruffly. She has posters of Jill Trenary, Rosalyn Sumners and Debbie Thomas all over the place. And since she's been skating pairs she's gotten a couple of posters of Gordeeva and Grinkov from the '88 Olympics, too,"

Beverly replied. "I know it's asking for disappointment but I do hope they make the Olympic Team next year."

There was a sudden sob, wrenched from deep down in her very soul. "It's so hard. This waiting. Not knowing. Dan is even more devastated than I am. We keep thinking we'll hear her voice, see her. Oh, not on the television but whenever the phone rings. Where is she?"

I didn't know what to say. How to comfort her or even if comfort was possible. How would I be feeling if it were our own well-beloved son? Terrible, lost and horribly lonely were only pale descriptions of how this couple were feeling.

Prosaically I said, "The bathroom's between this bedroom and the guest room next door. Come on in the family room when you're ready. We'll have a brandy—or hot chocolate if you'd rather."

Then I left the two of them to be together without an audience for a while.

The answering machine had been so busy it must have been dangerously close to overload. There were twenty one messages on it. I wearily got some paper and a pen, rewound it and started playing the tape. Most were from reporters and television stations wanting comments, statements and interviews. One rather rude male voice wanted to know what my thoughts had been while I was being choked and didn't I think broken fingers were a little drastic? Ghouls!

Our son had left a long message, none too polite, either. "Hey, Ma, where the hell are you? What's going on out there? Dad called me a little while ago. He's really worried. He says it sounds like you need a keeper. Are you two going to be able to come to my graduation? I need to know 'cause I have to buy you tickets. They're fifty dollars each so you'll have to send me a check for them. Well, I know you teach classes tomorrow but I'll call you at three in the afternoon. Be there, okay? 'Bye, talk to you tomorrow."

I replayed that message, taking notes of what he was going to catch it for when he did call. Ma—he'd never called me that in his life and it was too late for him to start now! And we'd need to pay fifty dollars a ticket to go to his graduation! Just who did he think paid those thousands of dollars a year for tuition? "Be there" as an order! Just wait 'til he called. I'd "Ma" him along with other suggestions of basic manners which he had learned as a child and was obviously forgetting as his book learning increased.

The long list of messages was finished. A couple of lesson time changes were the only ones I needed to take care of and that could be done in the morning.

Beverly and Dan came in, looking freshly washed but with red noses and eyes.

"Sit down. No, Misty, off. Let the Tompsons have the couch." The dog got up and moved to her favorite end, curled up tightly and went back to sleep, obviously feeling she had complied with the request as far as necessary.

The two visitors actually laughed and sat down on the portion of the sofa Misty had alloted to them. I got each of us a balloon glass of brandy. We sat quietly for awhile, each with our own thoughts while the dog gently snored away.

"What do you two plan for tomorrow? We have the classes in the morning but I'll be home after about one. Do you want to come to the rink or would you rather stay here? If tomorrow is like today the deck would be a great place to have brunch."

"We'd rather stay here, if you don't mind, Berrien," Dan said. "We're from the Midwest and I'm not up to driving these windy roads so close to the ocean. It probably wouldn't bother me too much usually but we're both nervous wrecks right now."

"Okay, you two stay here and relax as much as you can. I'm sure we'll have good news on Sunday because Deputy Mather is going to be able to talk to Pike tomorrow. Mather is sure that Pike is mixed up in the kidnapping somehow."

"Oh, I hope so. The uncertainty is so heard to bear."

"Well, good night. Help yourself to anything you want. I'd better get to bed. That ballet number practice almost finished me tonight."

Chapter 16

Exhausted, I had slept through the night, not even realizing that I was sleeping alone. A loud engine pffting woke me up. We live fairly close to a nude beach and every red-blooded male who is allowed to solo an airplane cruises the coast when the weather is good, dragging by at five hundred feet over the tide line.

What this particular character was hoping to see at seven o'clock on a sunny but chilly day was beyond my powers of comprehension. I was, however, distinctly annoyed. We aren't that close to the desired beach. I got up and looked out past the deck. There was the plane, a little Cessna two seater, dragging a banner behind it. The message on the long, flimsy ribbon was imploring the ungodly to repent.

Well, the week hadn't started out very auspiciously and sure didn't look like ending any better. My companion was not in the bedroom. That was unusual. I searched around for slippers and robe, found them and went down the hall towards the family room and kitchen. A whirring sound came from the kitchen along with the delicious smells of nutmeg and cinnamon.

Beverly was at the kitchen counter mixing something in the blender. Dan and the dog were on the floor, nuzzling each other. Beverly had found the waffle maker, which in my house is stored on a bottom shelf of the least handy cabinet, far in the back. We were about to be treated to strawberry waffles and crisp bacon which was just beginning to perfume the kitchen.

"Good morning. Everything smells wonderful."

"I always fix a big breakfast on the weekends. It's sort of a tradition with us. With all the early morning skating and late dinners Dan has put up with over the years I felt like I should pamper him on Saturdays and Sundays. Besides, right now it allows me to keep busy," Beverly said.

"And I'm keeping Misty Joy company," Dan said as clearly as he could while having his face washed by a moist, pink tongue. "She stayed the whole night with us. Just flaked out on the floor. Every once in a while she'd get up and come over and give one of us a light kiss."

"She would. Most dogs know when their family are depressed or sick and they go on their very best, most loving behavior. At least that's what I've found with all our pets. Misty knew you needed some loving. You're the first people other than family that she's done that for."

Beverly was busily working between the waffle iron, coffee pot and frying pan. "While we're here and you're at the rink, can I do some laundry or cleaning for you?"

"Oh, heavens, no. Thank you but I don't want you working. That wasn't why I invited you here."

"Please, let me. I love to wax furniture. And floors, too. Dan says he can always tell when I've got something worrying me. All the floors, furniture and windows shine. I'd be glad to have something to do. It makes the time go faster. That's what was so frustrating about being at the hotel."

"Well, you twisted my arm. What sensible woman would refuse an offer of help around the dirty house? This place could use some tender, loving care. I keep the tops of things dusted but don't do too much else. And I always forget the top of the refrigerator. Hey, I can't see it!"

"Can Misty stay with us?" Dan asked. "She's a lot of company. And so sweet. We didn't have any pets once Tami started skating. It wouldn't have been fair to them to be alone so much. I always had dogs when I was growing up, though."

"Sure. She'll probably enjoy a day off. Particularly since Gillian isn't there to give her the dog candies she keeps for her. The college kids don't have a key to her desk so they can't get it for the dog. I usually take some bones for them to give her but I forgot them the last couple of weeks."

After eating more of everything than was good for my waistline and arteries, I left for the rink and Saturday morning classes. Three hours of classes. If felt sort of lonely without Misty riding shotgun beside me.

The rink was already crowded with the kids in the freestyle classes, all ready to whoop it up on the ice. Since they couldn't get on until at least one pro was on themselves, they were raising cain in the aisle. I wish I could figure out why children, whenever they are in groups of three or more, feel called upon to squeal at the top of their voices. It seems that the question would be a valid Ph.D. thesis for a sociologist or psychologist.

"Where's Misty?"

"Why don't you have Misty Joy?"

"Is Misty okay? She's not sick, is she?"

I was surrounded by a clutch of the Misty Joy fan club, obviously.

"Hey," said one young boy who only came in to class on Saturday, never to practice, "I only come here so I can play with Misty. I hate this sissy sport. Hey, Mom! I want to go home."

"Misty's fine. We have guests at home so I left her to keep them company. She'll be here next week." Detaching myself from the crowd of kids, I headed to the pros' room to get my skates on. David, Miki and Sheli were already there. He was filling the twins in on the latest developments that Etienne had given us the night before.

"How's your mother doing? Are you going to be able to have the funeral soon?"

"Mom is very busy being mom and also chief mourner for Uncle Tomaso. Honestly, you'd think they had been bosom buddies all their lives. We're having the services on Monday. Then she can go back to Sea Ranch. Whether she will or not is another question. She wanted to come this morning but we talked her out of it. We think," Sheli answered.

We all got out on the ice and were immediately inundated by kids. Big kids, little kids, and Denise. She sailed onto the ice as usual, predictable as always, with the blade guards still on. She had been doing the same thing every Saturday morning for well over a year. The coaches and kids had learned to leave a path for her slide. No matter how often she was reminded, she still forgot, except for one memorable Saturday morning.

I had been standing near the music system and saw her start out and yelled, "Denise, take your guards off." She did and skated onto the ice instead of skidding on her bottom. In a rush, I hurried onto the ice myself. Fortunately, from force of habit everyone had left Denise's path open. I needed it. My guards were still on!

After the obligatory twirls and swirls, the kids sorted themselves into their proper classes. Soon David, Miki, Sheli and I could be heard shouting instructions. If private students hated to warm up, the class skaters hated it more, thoroughly aided and abetted in their rebellion by the skaters who took both kinds of lessons. To them it was a waste of time. We finally got them all moving enough to stretch any stiff muscles and then began the separate classes.

The higher level freestyle class that included the multiple revolution jumps was on the far rink, by themselves. The one closest to the office we used for the lower level skaters. Even with those simpler jumps we frequently felt like matadors with fifty enraged bulls let loose at once in a toy bull ring.

We devoted the last fifteen minutes of the hour to working on the required foot-work for each separate group. Jumps and spins are fine but watching skating that has no intricate connecting steps is somewhat boring. The judges think so. Scott Hamilton always comes to my mind when talk gets around to fancy footwork. He has no equal. We didn't teach anything as difficult as his but were building the basic ideas, slowly.

The next hour was devoted to beginners, first timers through the fourth level of basic skating. Again we had a battle over warm-up exercises and stretching which we won but not without a struggle. In this group, we used the separate rink for the very beginners. Those classes were always the largest and of course, they were the least steady on their feet. They needed the extra space to feel more secure.

Finally, in the last hour came our Wee Ones, the children from three to six years old. Some were mere beginners, others more advanced but still too small to join the larger children for classes. These classes are either the bane of a pro's existence or their joy. Frequently both at the same time.

I had one class, a number of years ago, that had a complete range of abilities. One small child, Amber, was having a hard time grasping the concept of using her feet in an alternating fashion. She would plant her tiny left foot on the ice and use her right foot as a sort of paddle. This method of locomotion was slow and it would always take her a long time to get from one side of the rink to the other.

Another child in the class was quick at picking up everything. Her parents always brought her early and she watched the older kids intently. The result was that she wanted to try things her classmates wouldn't attempt, thank heavens. Furthermore, she liked to show off. Jill would occupy herself during the time it took Amber to get across the rink by trying to spin, or jump, always out in the center of the ice. One day when Amber and I reached the wall, Jill was still performing.

"Jill," I called, "come over here."

"Jill, now!"

"Jilly, get over here," exasperation in my voice.

Amber looked up at me. She had the most gorgeous green eyes I had ever seen. "Does she just drive you up a wall?" asked this tiny little four-year-old.

I had to laugh. I hadn't heard that expression since my own mother had used it on me. "Wherever did you get that question, Amber?" I asked as soon as I could stifle my laughing and wipe my eyes clear of tears.

"Oh, my mother says I do it to her all the time."

And then there are little boys. As a general rule very young male children are not as coordinated as very young female children. Their center of gravity seems to be lower and farther behind them, literally. Little boys around the age of three or thereabouts tend to simply lean back and sit down with great ease and frequency. They have a lot of trouble getting upright again, the low center of gravity fighting against the maneuver.

Fortunately, most parents do not bring their very young male offspring for skating lessons. The proportions of tiny tot ladies to tiny tot gentlemen is roughly twenty to one. It is not until the young males discover the sport of hockey that their interest is piqued. Then they realize that to be able to play that rugged, manly sport, they must learn to balance upright on two thin pieces of steel. Well, upright part of the time, anyhow. That's when they start to come to classes.

After the Wee One classes I had scheduled a rehearsal of the *Wizard of Oz* number which was designed so that most of the smaller children in the classes only had to skate the one program. In doing that I had fixed a problem backstage managers had to cope with in amateur ice shows for years. The little ones would go to sleep, in dressing rooms, on benches and in one evening show where I was backstage manager, on my feet, resulting in a spectacular fall for me. Trying to move a prop I tripped over the little one and fell through the curtain and into full view of the audience just as four spotlights swept the curtain area.

Etienne, the producer of that show, was not amused.

We let the kids rest while Miki made the ice. I went into the office. I had seen Mather go in during the last class and wondered what he wanted. Didn't the man ever have a day off?

"You got everyone's prints the other day," roared Etienne, obviously not in the best of moods.

"No, I didn't. We didn't get your ballet teacher's nor did we get the bodybuilder's. Neither one of them were here last Monday. Are either of them here now?"

"Yes."

"Where?"

"Upstairs."

"Will you please call them down here?"

"Oh, all right." Etienne punched the button for the dance studio. "Ariadne, can you come down for a moment, please? Oh, and tell Trick we need him, too. Thanks."

We could hear Trick clomping down the stairs in the clogs he habitually wore around the gym. Ariadne was quicker and lighter and burst into the office a few yards ahead of him.

"Yes? Oh, Berrien, would you like me to help with the little ones' rehearsal? I adore working with tiny children. It was always so much fun to do *The Nutcracker ballet.*"

"We sure could use some help. They scoot all over the place. We should have designed a grid that we could lower from the ceiling to hold them in position. Thanks. I'll see you on the ice."

Trick arrived in the office. He still looked as if he had been poleaxed. He saw the crowd and turned around to leave. "Er, I'll come back when everyone's not so busy."

"No, Mr. Brewster," Sean said. "You and Ariadne weren't around the other day. We need to get both your fingerprints."

The young man turned an unappetizing shade of puce. "Why do you need mine?"

"Just for elimination purposes," the deputy explained. "There were so many different ones that every set we can identify helps us so much more."

"Oh, if you have to, I guess it's okay."

"Trick, for heaven's sake. It's not going to hurt," I said. "Get it over with!"

The short, powerful-looking figure slumped down into a chair. "All right. But do hers first," he said ungraciously, flinging an overdeveloped arm in Ariadne's direction. "Did you all get fingerprinted?"

Etienne, obviously keeping a tenuous hold on his temper said, "Yes, Trick. On Monday. I can't imagine why you are being so difficult."

Mather's technician approached the ballet teacher. She held out her hands and allowed him to direct the fingers to the proper places. She was given a moist towelette and wiped her hands clean.

"I'll go get my skates on and be right with you, Berrien."

"Okay."

Next the fingerprint man directed his attention to the bodybuilder. "Honestly, it won't hurt. You didn't hear the little lady scream, did you?"

"No, of course not," Trick answered, still looking as if he were going to be sick at any minute. He allowed the technician to take his prints with obvious reluctance. Finally, after the lab man had struggled to get a good impression while Trick's hands were going limp with each attempt, the job was finished.

Mather said a polite, formal, "Thank you for your cooperation, Mr. Brewster. We appreciate it."

"All right, Trick. You can go back to your lessons, now. Thanks," Etienne said. The young man left the office slowly and walked up the stairs. "Now, what the hell is wrong with him?" exploded 'Tienne. "What a fuss over nothing!"

Mather's professional poker face gave none of his thoughts away as he and the county lab tech left the arena.

The chaos of a rehearsal was inflated one hundred times with fifty small children bouncing around. *Over the Rainbow* was playing on the sound system, ineffectually competing with the chatter of the kids. I pulled my police whistle from my jacket pocket and blew hard!

Only one little one cried this time. They were getting used to the whistle. I was going to have to find a new, more exotic noisemaker if I wanted any hope of controlling this batch until the show actually got produced.

The number would be complete with a yellow brick road (a long strip of yellow oilcloth with handpainted "bricks"), a Wicked Witch, Cowardly Lion, the whole cast of characters. Dorothy would have red sequined slippers and a recording of Halloween sounds had given me the thunder, lightning and winds of a real tornado. Right at the end of this program would come the Junior Drill Team, completely thrilled with rainbow-colored sequin-covered costumes, skating to a disco version of Over The Rainbow.

With Ariadne to help, the practice went well. We actually got through two whole run-throughs without many hitches. The Wizard remembered his choreography, which was a first. And Dorothy tripped over Toto in the first run-through but managed to miss him in the second, giving me hope for the future. All of the props were not in place yet, nor could I set up some fun special effects until the dress rehearsal of the whole show. Mrs. Simeon was busy making the Tin Man costume and had found the perfect headpiece for it at Portugal's general store, a large, old-fashioned tin funnel.

"Thank you all for being here today. I'll post the next rehearsal on the bulletin board by Wednesday. There won't be one next week, though. Have a great weekend."

Amid clamorous shouts of leave-taking by the kids, parents and grandparents or other relatives, I slipped into the office with Ariadne. "Again, thank you, Ariadne. You're terrific! I'll talk to Etienne about getting you some money for all this work."

"Oh, don't worry about that—this really is fun and besides, it will probably increase sign-ups for the dance classes. I'm down here being seen, instead of hiding upstairs where I'm just mysterious. I'm so used to the pressures of professional performances that this is a real treat. Your music is wonderful and what I saw of the costumes looked well-thought-out. By the way, what's going to happen for the Senior Octet costumes?"

"Oh, I sent those little ones back but they told me they couldn't get the adult sizes in time. Mrs. Simeon and I will go into San Francisco next week and see what we can find. Probably plain leotards, yards of black lace to make ruffles and a ton of sequins. We have time and Mrs. Simeon is a hard worker."

"I can sew sequins and beads on, if you need any extra help," the slender dancer offered.

"We may take you up on it. See you Monday."

After visiting the pros' room, I went by the office to say goodby to Etienne.

"Are you going to be here tomorrow?" he asked.

"I hadn't planned on it. Why?"

"It's the Sunday for the Bay Area Ice Dancing Club tomorrow morning. Don't you skate it sometime?"

"Yes, but Dan and Beverly are staying at the house. I don't think it's nice to leave them alone again."

"I'm supposed to go to dinner in Berkeley tonight with friends and I'll probably stay over until tomorrow. Could you just come in and open the rink? I'll get a couple of skate guards to be here during the session."

"Okay. Sure. Have a nice time. Oh, we're supposed to hear from Tami or her kidnapper tomorrow. Have you heard anything from the FBI? Did they find out any more about where she might be?"

"Yes. They're sure she's being kept in San Francisco. But just where, they don't have any idea yet."

"Are you sure Mather and those people are all staying in touch with each other?"

"I'm sure they are. Everyone is convinced the murder of Uncle Tomaso and Tami's kidnapping are related. How are the Tompsons doing?"

"Well, Beverly cooked us a huge breakfast this morning. Then when I left she was getting out cleaning supplies. Says it'll take her mind off the fear for a little while. I think I'll stop and get some steaks. We could grill them on the deck and ocean watch." I looked at my watch. "Hey, I'd better get on my way. Trent called yesterday and ordered—get that ordered—me to be home at three o'clock so we can talk. If he's that bossy now, I'm afraid he's going to be unbearable as soon as he gets that degree. I'm going to have to take him down a few pegs."

"Take care. At least you don't have to worry about Pike. He's out of the cardiac care unit but is still listed in serious condition. Both Sean and the FBI people are going to finally be allowed some time with him today."

"I wonder how he's doing mentally, now? Well, I guess we'll find out soon."

The Portugal General Store was crowded with shoppers who came from up and down the Coast to get meat for the weekend. They had Harris Ranch beef and free-range chickens all the time. The ecology and animal activists loved to shop there for that reason. I loved it because the meat was so good. I got the steaks and some vegetables that had been picked so recently they were still warm from the sun.

I opened the door to the wonderful smells of freshly polished furniture, spotless waxed floors and bunches of tulips and marguerites just cut from the side yard that greeted me. Our beautiful house gleamed proudly. Dan and Beverly were sitting out on the deck, the portable phone on the table between the two chairs. They were clutching mugs of coffee in one hand so tightly their knuckles were white. The other hands were entwined. Misty Joy lay on the deck, stretched out to cover all four feet.

Dumping the groceries on the spotless countertop, I went outside. "Did you get any phone calls? What's happened?" I asked.

"No, we thought we'd better keep the phone with us, though. I hope you don't mind," Dan said. "It hasn't rung even once."

"Of course not. Let me go put the groceries away. I thought we could grill some steaks out here tonight. And I got some really fresh greens for a salad, too. I'll be right back." My faithful mutt didn't even bother to lift her head.

By now it was close to three and Trent's call would come in any minute. I poured myself a cup of coffee and went out to join the Tompsons. The little plane was long gone. I sure hoped it wouldn't show up on Sunday but maybe the pilot would be busy in church.

"This certainly is a lovely home and a marvelous setting," Beverly said. "I love hearing the ocean. It's so soothing, timeless. We've been watching the ships out in the water. There aren't a whole lot, though, are there?"

"No, you don't see too many anymore. I bet it was something else during Prohibition. Someone told me once that this stretch of coastline was a primary landing area for the rumrunners. There were Coast Guard boats swooping up and down the coast trying to stop the trade. A lot was off-loaded, at least so I'm told, right at that jetty you can see from the rink."

"Well, the Great Lakes had a lot of traffic from Canada, too. I've heard stories all my life about trips to Canada to buy the booze. Some just did it for family but there were apparently a lot of people who brought more back to sell. I'm glad I didn't live in those days. Imagine, friends and family casually breaking the law!" Dan remarked.

The phone rang just then. He handed me the portable. My son's voice came over the line. "Hi, Ma!"

"What's with 'Ma'? You've never used that term before yesterday! At least not within my hearing. And you can stop using it right now."

"Aw, I'm just trying to cheer you up. Or use shock treatment. It's a good thing I'm going in for orthopedics. Those psychology terms always did confuse me."

"I don't need cheering up, you ungrateful pup. And what about the tickets for graduation? When do you have to pay for them? And are you going to get us a hotel room, too? Your dad and I are not, repeat not, going to stay in the pigpen you and your roommates live in."

"Hey, you've always got dirt deep enough to grow potatoes in on top of the refrigerator. Since when did you get so fussy?"

"Since I walked into the house this afternoon and it is the cleanest, sparklyist house in the country."

"What's going on, Ma—I mean Mother?"

"Tami's parents are staying with me for awhile and Beverly cleaned this morning. The place looks and smells like an ad for *Architectural Digest*. You wouldn't recognize it."

"That's great. Now. Seriously. Are you all right? I read in the sports page about Vaughan Pike trying to choke you."

"Yes, I'm fine, Trent. My throat is bruised but it's fading. You can't blame him, not too much. He's really ill and I won't discuss that further on this phone."

"Of course he's sick. He had a heart attack. Is he going to be okay? I would have loved to have seen his face when Sheli broke his fingers! He's such a pain in the butt about how delicate ladies are."

"He's recovering from the surgery but he hasn't been able to be interviewed yet. They were going to do it this afternoon. Maybe we'll know everything by tomorrow. I sure hope so. Another week like this one and my hair will be pure white."

"I'm glad you have company. Dad was really worried when we talked a couple of days ago. When's he get home?"

"Monday."

"Good. How's the show coming?"

"Not too badly. The usual problems but we're getting it finished. Costumes aren't all here, though and pictures are scheduled for ten days from now. Oh, well, we'll work it out."

"Sounds normal for you and Etienne. I'm glad I'll get to see this one, M-Mom. Make sure you have film for the camcorder. I'll tape it for you."

"Okay. Sounds good."

"Oops. Look at the time. I'm on duty in the ER tonight and tomorrow. I'll call Monday night so I can talk to Dad, too."

"By, Sonny." That would put a stop to "Ma."

Beverly said, "It sounds like you two have a good feeling about one another. Is he married?"

"No, Philip and I told him we could support his medical school or his wife, but not both. Med school is hard on everyone concerned and particularly marriages. He's got his internship to get through and then the residency training, all involving long hours and low pay. He can't afford a wife right now. Besides, I'd kind of like it if he and Sheli were to get together. 'Course, that's what I'd like. They get along well as friends but I don't think there's any spark between them."

"Yes, I know I want Tami to be happy in her life after skating but we can't dictate to our children. We made our decisions and they have to learn to make theirs, mistakes and all. But I really believe that skaters are better equipped for adult life than the young ones without any interests while they are growing up. Our kids are sheltered in one way but know that they have to work for what they want."

"I agree, as long as the parents aren't using their children to fulfill their own dreams. Every time I see a skater yelled at by mom or dad, or a coach because they didn't skate perfectly in a competition I get furious. Ice is slippery stuff, anyone can have a bad day and when some parents start degrading the skater, in public, it is devastating to the kid. And I've seen it in the lowest levels of competition. That's not right. 'Win. Yes, if you can, but just get out and do your very best. Then I'll be proud of you' is what I like to tell my skaters. It's not a bad thing to learn at a young age that you don't always get what you want and even what you might deserve."

Dan and Beverly thought that over for a moment. "I see what you mean. The skaters always try hard—and work awfully hard with discipline not many adults have. They shouldn't be berated, even in private, if they don't win a medal but praised for being out there," Dan said reflectively. "And I've seen some of the behavior you're talking about, too. That was one of the good things about Mr. Pike. He always gave his skaters hugs and praise. At least he used to. What a terrible thing this unspeakable disease is doing to him!"

"How did you start skating, Berrien?" Beverly asked, trying to change the subject.

"I always wanted to but there were no rinks where I grew up. I only skated on ponds in the winter. After I got out of college I moved to a city that had one. Started skating and talk about embarrassing! Skating preliminary figures and learning waltz jumps as an adult when these tiny little things are whipping around complicated loops and brackets and doing double jumps. I really felt like an idiot but stuck to it because I love the sport so much. There's not much call for thirty-year-olds in competition so I turned pro and started teaching. It's a fun, if sometimes exasperating, way to earn a living. Sure beats a chemistry lab."

"Sounds like you really wanted to skate."

"Oh, I did. Well, let me get the grill started and go in and do something with all the rabbit food I bought for a salad."

"It's so nice out here we can even eat here."

"Let's. But you or Dan'll have to stay here when the steaks are cooking. Our furry friend here has been known to try to get one off the barbecue. I don't want her to get burned. Even if she has deserted me for you guys. You should have heard the kids today wanting to know where she was."

The wind was beginning to kick up a bit and the fog was coming closer in to shore. It wouldn't be too long before it would be downright chilly. I started the fire for the steaks and wrapped some potatoes in foil then went into the kitchen to wash the salad fixings. Beverly followed me.

"Here, let me do that."

We worked in a companionable silence. I gathered plates, utensils and condiments together and took them outside to set the table. The sky was garish as the setting sun tinged wisps of white clouds a flamingo pink with a pale blue background that was changing slowly to indigo in the East.

The potatoes were baking, the steaks were marinating in a sauce that Trent claimed he had invented. I rather suspected that he had gotten the recipe from a friend's mother, but who was I to quibble? Time for drinks. We had all earned them, given the week we had just been through. And there was still tomorrow. We had no idea of how, when or where the kidnapper planned to make contact with the rink, the Sheriff's office or the FBI.

Dan, Beverly and I sat looking out over the ocean, sipping our martinis. These were such nice people. What a shame such a horrible experience was making their enjoyment of Tami's success as a skater seem more of a nightmare.

"Do you wish Paul and Tami hadn't won the title?"

"No. No. Never that. It was a wonderful thing. They were so happy. So were we, of course. And surprised. Were you at Nationals?"

"No. I just got to see it on the television program. They did a marvelous program. And the new lift Miki and Sheli invented for them will really set them apart. I wouldn't have tried it when I was a kid!"

Dinner was over and the sun had set spectacularly between the incoming fog bank and the brightly painted sky. Just as it was disappearing toward Hawaii, we saw an elegant, enormous sailboat heading north toward San Francisco. A gorgeous sight.

Chapter 17

Suddenly Dan asked, "Do you think we could go to the hospital to see Mr. Pike? It seems really nasty not to see how he's doing, maybe visit with him a bit. He's probably bored and lonely. No friends out here to visit with."

"Why don't we call the hospital and see if he can have company?" I suggested. "If Sean Mather and the FBI people were in to see him today, he's probably exhausted."

"If you wouldn't mind driving us, we'd really rather just take our chances at seeing him. After all, he was Tami's coach for a long time. If he knows we're out here in California, he'll feel badly not to see us."

"But Sean thinks he's mixed up in Tami's kidnapping. Are you sure you want to go?"

"Yes, we were talking about it before you came home but we didn't know the way to the hospital and I really don't want to drive on this road very much. We'd really appreciate it."

"Okay, I'll take you but I don't think I'd better let him see me. He seems to get manic when he spots me."

We cleared the dishes away and made sure the fire in the grill was out. I simply dumped water into the charcoal, not the recommended procedure but the fastest. Then we piled in my car, including Misty Joy, who claimed her co-pilot seat in the front. I hoped neither of the Tompsons got car sick on winding roads.

The fog was beginning a swift approach from its daily perch somewhere out on the horizon. We drove through Half Moon Bay, crowded with Saturday night visitors, the parking lots at capacity and no parking left on the streets, either. I glimpsed only two of the mobile TV vans with their antennas and circular dishes. Maybe there would not be any clamor when Tami was returned tomorrow. I refused to think of "if."

Carmichael Hospital Coastside is an adjunct of a large trauma center on the Peninsula. It has a superb emergency capacity with specially trained emergency personnel who have been taught to handle major disasters, especially water-related problems. There is a helipad on the property and if necessary patients are transported by air to the parent hospital quickly.

Pike's heart attack, however, had been so sudden and so severe there had not even been time for him to be flown over the hill. The cardiovascular surgeon at Coastside and his team had done a wonderful job. Sean had said earlier that Pike had been taken from the small CCU and put into a private room.

We parked close to the front door and went in. The reception desk was empty, as were the billing office and the admitting area. It wasn't unusual. On a Saturday night most of the action would be at the emergency room as the barbecue brigade came in with burns of varying degrees of severity and the automobile accident victims were toted in with everything from minor cuts to major traumas.

The elevator took us to the second floor and we stepped out into a well-lighted waiting room. Visitors and patients were walking around. The patients were pretty well identifiable by their accompanying stands with fluids dripping from plastic bags through long plastic tubes into their human targets. We heard snatches of conversations. Almost everyone was gathered at the far end of the large, airy room, sitting in well-pillowed, white wicker furniture. They were watching the traffic on the Pacific Coast Highway and the white froth on the waves just beyond. A full moon made the ocean seem magical as it surged back and forth with the pull of the tide.

Despite the lovely view, it smelled like a hospital, though. That force-fed cleanliness, combined with the odors of illness, urine and fear was there.

We headed toward the rear of the hallway where I knew the private rooms were. The nurses' station was empty. I had seen several aides with the patients and the visitors in the waiting room and wondered where the nurses were. We passed by several empty rooms, no doubt the wave-watchers temporary residences. From the far end of the hall we could hear two loud male voices. Not at all what is to be expected in a hospital where hushed conversations were always the norm.

Bells dinged, requests for doctors or nurses to call other doctors or nurses or the lab boomed over the loudspeakers. We looked briefly into each room as we hurried along. I was letting the Tompsons go ahead of me so that I could avoid having the skating coach see me. The hallway made an abrupt left turn. We could see that these were the private rooms on the left side of the hall. Each one had a view of the ocean.

The voices were either getting louder or we were much closer to them. I couldn't recognize either of them. In between the bursts of shouting, a fainter, mewling sound could be heard. It sounded as if someone had snuck a kitten into a patient's room.

We could begin to distinguish words now as we came closer to the last room on the left side of the corridor.

"You miserable bastard! You swore to me you didn't have it! And now I find out you do," screamed a voice I thought I recognized. "And I've given it to Vernon! We're both positive!"

The second loud voice bellowed, "We're gonna die. Because of you. You shouldn't have lied to Richard. I'd like to kill you!"

The scratchy kitten sounded again but we couldn't hear the words clearly. Suddenly Dan stopped short and I skidded into his back. The door to the last room was open. We could see the backs of two men standing over the bed. Vaughan Pike lay in the bed, pale as the immaculate white sheet pulled up to his chin. Several stands containing life-giving fluids dripped into his arms. He was hooked up to several monitors although he only had one of those little nose-clips to deliver extra oxygen to him. I could see the green lines of the monitors doing a violent dance, bouncing from the top to the bottom of the screens and then repeating the process.

Pike looked from one man to the other, eyes pleading, fearful. Suddenly, the one called Richard raised his arms and brought massive fists down on Pike's chest. He kept pounding, pounding. Vernon tried to pull him away as bells went off at the nurses' station.

We could hear the Code Blue call over the loudspeakers. A nurse came skidding around the corner pushing a cart loaded with gadgets and medicines. "Out of my way. Who are you? What are you doing here?" she gasped as she sped by.

There was sudden quiet as the bells and whistles stopped their cacophony. The two men, one short, husky and vaguely familiar, the other tall, gangly, wearing what appeared to be black ballet tights, shoved the nurse and her heavy cart out of their way and raced for the emergency stairs just a few feet away from the door to Pike's room.

The cart careened off the wall, bouncing into Dan, knocking him into the metal fire extinguisher housing. He fell to the floor with a low moan and then lay still. The heavy piece of life-saving equipment next attacked Beverly, sending her sprawling on the floor. It then rolled over one of her legs and stopped finally, pinning her down. I heard a sickening snap as the bones in her lower left leg shattered.

A doctor, answering the Code Blue, rushed around the corner. "What's going on here? Why are you two on the floor?"

Deputies, waiting for accident victims to recover consciousness in the emergency room plunged around the corner not far behind the doctor. I pointed to the emergency door. "Two men, one short and husky, the other taller, skinny, wearing black ballet tights went down those stairs. They had been in Mr. Pike's room." The policemen slammed open the door and clattered down the metal steps.

Soon, more medical personnel were pouring into the hallway. Patients and visitors, drawn by the commotion, were peering around the turn.

The medical staff was working on Dan and Beverly. One of the aides shooed the patients to their rooms and the visitors out the door. Dan was groaning, trying to sit up. Blood was dribbling from a cut just above his ear where he had caught the supposedly recessed door handle. His eyes were unfocused but he kept trying to look for Beverly.

She was shaking with shock, pain and fear. "My leg hurts. Oh, it hurts so! Where's Dan?"

The cart was lifted carefully over Beverly's leg by two large, healthy-looking orderlies. A doctor squatted down and gently felt around. There was an ugly white stick visible through her stocking, the blood turning it a pinky color not unlike the hues of the clouds we had been watching so recently.

"I'm Doctor Givens," a young, red-haired man introduced himself. "Let me take a look at these two. What happened here?"

"How is Pike?" I asked.

"Dead. I don't understand it. I checked him just two hours ago. He was doing much better than I had hoped."

The two orderlies arrived with two gurneys. They carefully lifted Beverly onto one, bracing her left leg carefully, ready to take her to X-ray. Dan was helped onto a matching conveyance, headed in the same direction. They were holding hands.

Another deputy got out of the elevator. It was Jonathan Martin again. He turned to watch the Tompsons loaded onto the elevator, startled when he recognized them as a part of the skating family.

"Berrien. What's going on? Wasn't that the Tompsons, Tami's parents, on those carts?"

"Yes. We came up to see Vaughan. Or rather I brought them up. I wasn't going to go in. They've known him a long time and wanted to say hello. They're nice people and felt he might like to see a friendly face. But we got here to this—this mess!" I wailed. I'm not generally the wailing kind but the past week had gotten to me.

Doctor Givens came over and led me to the waiting rooms, now deserted by everyone except one patient. It was an old man, sitting in one of the wicker chairs. He had obviously left his false teeth in his room, his lips and cheeks were sunken. He needed a shave, white whiskers were poking out of the seams in every crevice of his face. He was muttering to himself.

Jonathan sat down opposite me as I took one of the thickly pillowed chairs facing out to the ocean. "Okay, Berrien, I don't understand anything of what's happening. Had I better call Sean Mather?"

"Pike's dead. There were two men in his room, yelling at him. Then the one called Richard started pounding on his chest. It was awful!"

"Hitting his chest," said Givens. "That could be...was fatal. Fright, pain or just physical destruction of the sutures, anyone of those could have killed him."

The deputy went to the nurses' station to call his office. He didn't know what the procedure was going to be. After all the man had died in a hospital.

He came back to us. Doctor Givens was sitting with me. We were both staring out at the moonlit ocean.

"Doctor Givens," said Jonathan, "the body will have to go to the coroner's department for an autopsy. The problem with that is he had such major surgery only a few days ago. The coroner asked if you would be able to give him some help. He'll call you to set a time at your convenience but he said that he'll really need some guidance on injuries as opposed to the surgical bruises."

"Of course, I'll be glad to be of service. I'm appalled that something so gruesome could occur in my hospital—any hospital for that matter. Just have him give me a call. Here's my card with all my numbers on it except the home one. Here, let me write that one down on the back."

"Thanks. I'll need to talk to Berrien now, and to the Tompsons as soon as possible. How are they doing?"

The doctor got up. "Let me go downstairs and check on them. I'll be back in a few minutes."

"Thanks."

"Okay, Berrien. Mather will be here in a half an hour. Poor guy, they had a baby-sitter already there and dinner reservations. His wife was ranting loud enough for me to hear her over the phone."

"Do you want to ask any questions now or wait until Sean gets here? Could we go out to the car? I need to let Misty out and get her some water, too, if we're going to be here for much longer."

"Sure, I could do with a walk myself."

Just then the two deputies who had chased after the two men came into the waiting room. They spotted Jonathan and walked over to us just as we were getting up. One was movie-star handsome, a Denzil Washington look-alike. The other was shorter, dark brown curly hair and a face that was only now becoming smooth after years of serious acne which must have caused him incredible pain, both physically and emotionally.

"We saw a van leave the parking lot, headed up the Coast toward Pacifica. We think those men were in it but can't be sure. They had too much of a head start. Their car was right at the edge of the parking lot. It took us a while to get the cruiser. By the time we got on the road it was too late. They'd disappeared, there were too many cars between us," said Ronnie, the Denzil clone. "It was too far away even to get a plate number, but it was an old Ford van, dark in color, blue, brown, black maybe. Not much help, I'm afraid."

"Okay, write out a report on it anyway. At this point anything'll be a help. They'll probably be charged with Pike's murder."

"Pike who?" asked the younger deputy whose name plate identified him as Albert.

"It's that skating coach who's gotten all the publicity this week," answered Jonathan. "Oh, hell. I hope nothing about this has gone out over the radio! There're still those TV people in Half Moon Bay."

"We didn't use the radio. We barely left the parking lot before we realized it would only endanger too many other drivers without giving us much chance of catching that van. If we'd been sure it was the right one we might have tried but we didn't know for sure."

"Okay. I'm sure Mather will want to talk to you but you'd better get going now. The Saturday night drunks are waiting," Jonathan encouraged. "Okay, Berrien. Let's go take your mutt for her walk. Does she like the beach?"

"Of course. But she's not going there tonight. She'd need a bath when we got home. Somehow, I feel that I'm going to be much too tired to give her one."

We got Misty out of the car. She greeted me happily and then turned to give Jonathan a kiss. We walked across the highway and turned to the right along a pathway just above the beach. The moon was still fighting to be seen. The fog was going to win the battle shortly but for now we could still see the waves curling into shore. I love the ocean in its many moods. And love to swim in it. However, up around the San Francisco Bay the Pacific Ocean is so cold that only certifiably crazy surfboarders in full wet suits or card-carrying members of the local Polar Bear Club spend much time actually in the water.

After the stroll, I locked Misty back in the car, hospitals not being much on four-legged creatures as visitors and we went back upstairs to the now familiar waiting room. Sean had arrived.

"Berrien, I think I need to lock you up and throw away the key. Just for the safety of the Coast residents!"

"Sean, that's not funny." I have a pretty good sense of humor but that was too close to the way I was really feeling.

"Okay, okay. I'm sorry. Now, tell me what happened tonight. Start from the beginning."

I related all that had happened since the Tompsons and I had walked into the hospital. After I had finished, Mather, of course, had some questions.

"Can you describe these men?"

"Not very well. I was behind Dan and Beverly. I could see that it was Pike in the bed, and all those monitors. They faced the door. I guess so the nurses can look at them quickly. The two men had their backs to the door. One was called Richard. He's fairly short, very muscular, had a baseball cap on. He's the one who beat on Pike. The other guy is tall and skinny. He has really skinny legs. I could see because he either had on shrink-to-fit jeans that had already been shrunk or they were ballet tights. Big feet, black sneakers large enough to use as a rowboat. He's bald on top with a fringe of long hair that I could swear looked blue, long in back in a pony tail. He must have been Vernon."

"Did you see their faces? Could you recognize them again?"

"No. I didn't see their faces. Their backs were toward us and when they rushed out everything seemed to happen at once, what with the nurse screaming, the cart doing the cha-cha and bodies rolling on the floor. I just saw their backs again as they ran to that emergency door. The one called Richard—his voice sounded sort of familiar but it had so much hate, I guess is what I want to say, in it that I don't really know who it reminded me of."

"Anything else you can think of?"

"No. I think I've told it all. Can we find out how Dan and Beverly are doing? Then I'd like to go home."

"Let's go down to the nurses' station. They might be able to tell us."

Just then the elevator doors opened and two gurneys rolled out. My two friends were still holding hands. We walked over to them. They were both drowsy, Beverly from the anesthesia she had had while the bones were set and the cut where the bone had slashed through was repaired. Dan, of course, was groggy from the concussion he had suffered. We followed them down the hall and into the room assigned to them.

A nurse came in. "Don't tire them out. Mrs. Tompson will be here for several days. We need to keep her husband overnight, at least, to check him out. Can you stop by the desk and give me some information on them, please?"

"Of course, we'll do that now. Good night you two, I'll be by in the morning."

At the desk I tried as best I could to answer the usual bureaucratic questions and explained the situation to the nurses.

Sean and Jonathan added that they had better be ready to repulse the media. Sean said, "As soon as they learn about this fracas they'll be trying to talk to the Tompsons. If I can, I'll get a deputy to guard them tonight."

"Thanks. None of the patients need anymore excitement tonight. There's one patient, though, who keeps calling for the police. He says he saw something you need to know. Heavens knows what some of the others are thinking."

"Would you like us to go see the patient who keeps calling for the police. If he can say his piece, it might help him sleep."

"Oh, could you? He's usually pretty sharp but I don't know if he has anything for you. But it would put his mind at ease. Thanks."

She led the way to another private room on the ocean side. The fog had won the battle and we could barely see the highway with the light beams from the passing cars looking filmy and unsubstantial.

"Mr. Packer, this is Deputy Mather and Deputy Martin. Would you like to talk to them?"

"License plate. I saw a van with two men in it. Got the plate number."

Mr. Packer was the old gentleman who had been sitting in the waiting room while Jonathan and I had been talking before Mather arrived. Jonathan said, "Please, it would be a big help, Mr. Packer."

"It was AB 164. Here, I wrote it down on a piece of paper when I got back here," he said as he gave a flimsy piece of tissue to Mather.

"Could you see what state the plate was from?"

"Why, it's a California plate, young man. We're in California. It was a white plate with dark numbers. Yes, definitely a California plate."

"Well, thank you very much, Mr. Packer. We appreciate your help."

We left Mr. Packer's room before saying anything more. Unless it was a vanity plate of some kind, it was not a California license. Mather said, "Well, I'd better call it in, anyhow. It could be one of any number of states but it's sure not one of ours. I wish he had gotten the make of the van."

"I don't see how he could have gotten the number. That place where the deputies said they were parked is quite a distance. I'd have a hard time seeing that there was even a plate there, never mind reading it," I commented.

"Why are you still here, Berrien? I know you have a home. Go!" ordered Mather. "We don't need you anymore."

"What a gracious statement, Deputy. Although now you mention it, it's a great idea. Good night."

We were standing in the waiting room again. Just as I said that, the entrance to the hospital was impaled with megawatt lights. The parking lot was a maze of cables running from the big TV vans that had been so cozily parked back in Half Moon Bay several hours ago. Someone had been listening to a police radio.

"Oh, shit," Jonathan swore. "Come on, Berrien. Let's get you to your car before they recognize Misty Joy. We'll get you out the back road. Then go straight home and stay there."

"Yes, sir!"

Jonathan led the way while Mather stayed upstairs, hoping to be able to talk, at least for a short time, with one or both of the Tompsons. We went out through the kitchens and got to my car without attracting any attention. He told me how to get to the service road and went back into the hospital.

Misty, happy to see me, and even more pleased to be in a moving, as opposed to stationary, vehicle, stood up in the seat, wagging her tail. She might just as well have hung her head out the window to say, "Hi, I'm over here."

Fortunately, I was already moving and drove through the onrushing journalists without getting stopped as we headed for home.

Chapter 18

I tossed and turned restlessly. Misty Joy retreated to her own bed in disgust. The events of the evening ran ceaselessly through my mind like The Gong Show on a never-ending tape. Why couldn't I remember who that voice reminded me of?

Finally, as daylight began to show in the east, I got up and went to the family room and made some coffee. Misty followed me and fell asleep on the couch. I still had to go to the rink to open it for the Bay Area Ice Dancing Club. That is a loosely formed club who skate a couple of times a week at the various rinks in the San Francisco Bay area. They like to go to different rinks but they don't come to *N'ice Skates* too often. It is a little out of the way to get to and a long drive for some of the skaters early on a Sunday morning.

The advertising machine that was the Sunday paper was waiting on the front steps when I opened the door. Screaming headlines announced the death of Vaughan Pike and the injuries to the Tompsons. I could hardly wait until Etienne saw that.

I took the paper and my coffee outside with the dog. The article was highly colored with suppositions and was extremely sketchy on facts, including as it did descriptions of masked men and gunfire in a hospital corridor. Where in the world did they get information like that? This writer should try her hand at fiction. Maybe that's what she really wanted to be when she grew up.

A quick call to the hospital told me that Beverly was doing as well as could be expected, whatever that phrase means, and Dan could be released about eleven. The doctor needed to check him one more time. I told the nurse on duty that I would come pick him up by noon.

It was another glorious Spring day on the Coast. Gentle breezes, mere wisps of clouds, the heavy fog of the night before was dissipated in the morning sunshine. I cut some tulips and packed them in soggy paper to take to Beverly later.

Standing in the fitted closet, I had to decide if I were going to skate the dance session. If so, I needed to struggle into a skating dress. They may look pretty on the ice but even practice dresses are a real pain in the butt to get on—and off when nature calls. After all the food I had been eating all week, I decided skating was a necessity and got into a black, floral print number, then pulled on a lightweight jogging outfit over it that would be acceptable garb at the hospital later.

"No, Misty Joy. You stay home. Too many people get on and off the ice during dance. I don't want to haul you off four or five times like I did last month."

The big, white dog got "that look" on her face. For such a normally sweet-tempered animal she can be remarkably stubborn. That's when I call her "muleface." The head lowers and she stares up at me without blinking. Normally, I let her have her way then. This time I couldn't. At the last dance session we had gone to, she had gotten out onto the ice during a fast march, almost tripped a couple who are in their seventies, just missed getting spiked by a swinging blade and knocked me into the wall.

The short drive to the arena was pleasant, still too early in the morning for much traffic, just a couple of cars with some of the dance group heading in my direction. There was one fancy, sporty Porsche speeding north toward Half Moon Bay which passed us. We all turned into the parking lot.

Already there was an old van, rusty, dark brown. It had certainly seen better days but not recently. There were no license plates on it that I could see. I would have to have it hauled away.

I unlocked the door to the rink, thinking back to Monday morning and the unlocked door. Both ice surfaces gleamed, smooth and inviting. It was possible to use both rinks and either have a much larger dance session than usual or allow pros to give lessons on one surface while others were enjoying the social dancing on the other. Unlike a lot of arenas, we allowed pros who weren't attached to *N'ice Skates* to give lessons during the Sunday morning dance session. It was good publicity and good public relations. Sneakily, it allowed me to recruit a lot of dancers for a dance number in the show.

David and I had concocted a wonderful number that would be attached to the ballet waltz program. Rehearsals for that were scheduled for next Sunday with twelve couples signed up for it.

More of the skaters came in. "Hey, Berrien, who owns that rust bucket out there?" asked Harold Barker, one of the regulars. "That looks like a reject from the Haight in the sixties."

"Thanks for reminding me. I'd better call the Sheriff's department. Again. They must be getting really tired of us by now."

The two skate guards arrived, yawning, with two huge boxfuls of doughnuts and a couple of gallon jugs of chilled orange juice.

"You guys aren't going to eat those all, are you?" I asked.

"No. Etienne asked us to bring them in for the group. He gave us money last night. We stopped at the bakery. The doughnuts are still warm. Help yourself."

We set them, the juice, some cups and plates on the skate counter for everyone to serve themselves. Soon there was a crowd around the counter. Then, one of the guards got the music system going. We all stampeded to the ice. The first few dances were low test, easy, deliberately so because we were all as bad about proper warm-up as the kids.

Pleasantly tired, sweaty and disheveled, we finished at eleven. Goodbys were said. "Don't forget next Sunday's rehearsal for the show," I called to the twenty-four victims, er, twelve couples who had volunteered for duty.

As we went out to the parking lot, a county-hired tow truck was lifting the front end of the old van, getting ready to cart it off to wherever rusted old vans go.

"Wait a minute!" shouted a muscular man, obviously in charge of the tow truck. "I thought I heard something in there."

We all listened intently. I could only hear the waves as they slapped against the rocks below us. Then a faint sound of a cry, weak but human came again. "Help. Let me out."

Ted, the tow truck man, pounded on the van's wall. "Is someone in there?"

Again, "Help me!" the voice was stronger now.

Ted ran quickly to his truck's tool box and came back with a crowbar. He forced it into the back doors and pried it open. The entire dance group stood by, speechless, breathless. He climbed into the van and soon came out, carrying a girl, tied up, with her face scratched from rubbing the duct tape off her mouth. The tape was still dangling from her right cheek, tangled in the mess of hair.

"Tami!" I screamed as we all recognized the girl.

David hurried over to help the driver as they set her down gently. They unwound the tape holding her arms behind her and keeping her legs together.

I went in to call, yet again, first the Sheriff's office and then the hospital for an ambulance and also to tell the doctors to let Dan and

Beverly know that Tami was alive, apparently unharmed and would soon be arriving at the hospital, herself.

"I'm thirsty. Could I have some water, please?" Tami asked.

One of the guards went in and got some orange juice, brought it out in a cup, along with the rest of the bottle. "Would you like a doughnut?" he asked.

"Yes, please. They didn't feed me today. They just tied me up and drove over winding roads, it seemed like forever. I've got bruises on my bruises." She wolfed down a huge apple fritter in a matter of seconds.

"Tami," I asked, "who had you? Where were you? Do you know?"

Before she could answer the now familiar sound of an ambulance rushing on its way to *N'ice Skates* came well in advance of the vehicle itself. It was not the only one, either. One lone TV truck followed it. They both slid to a stop just short of the group standing around.

"Where's the patient?" shouted the paramedic. "I hope I don't have to get out on that ice again."

"No. She's right here," I said and pointed to Tami, who was by now sitting on the top step of the entrance to the rink. Sugar glaze from the apple fritter had been added to the mix of adhesive, scratches and filthy hair. She was not an appealing picture. Her jeans, shirt and once-sky-blue sweater bore the signs of a week of hard wear.

The TV crew had, by now, hopped out of their van and were busily filming the scene, one which was going to thrill the powers that be in figure skating to no end. The young lady who had tried to destroy my teeth earlier in the week was advancing, microphone again at the ready, on Tami.

David, normally quiet and camera-shy, took charge of the scene by standing in front of the camera, holding his hand over the lens of the hand-held mini-cam. "Leave her alone! We will arrange for an interview after she has been checked out at the hospital. Now, GO!"

The young woman, anxious to have her time in the spotlight and a future chance at an anchor job, immediately began to bleat about her

First Amendment rights. If David hadn't been a gentleman—as well as a gentle man—the announcer would have been handed her own teeth in a bag. As it was, her cameraman, worried about damage to expensive equipment, started to back off as the group of ice dancers began to surge around Tami to protect her.

A big Cadillac pulled in and a crazy man got out of the car, leaving the engine running. Etienne was back and bellowing in French. None of us understood a word he was saying. The camera operator swung around and got some footage of 'Tienne in full rage, complete, I was sure, with sound. I hoped it was going to have to be bleeped out.

"Etienne! Calm down! Tami's here. She's okay. She's going to the hospital to be checked out and to see her Mom and Dad. I've already called there to tell them she's fine."

"Please, Etienne, I'm okay. Honest. What do you mean I'll see Mom and Dad at the hospital? Why are they here? What's been going on? Where's Paul?"

"Good grief! I forgot to call him. I'll do it as soon as you get out of here, Tami. A deputy named Sean Mather will meet you there. He'll get your story and I'll be there soon."

Finally, she climbed into the ambulance under her own power and it left the arena parking lot in a hurry. David, Etienne and I went into the rink.

"We have to call Paul. Oh, and Miki and Sheli, too. They'll be so relieved."

"And what is this about Vaughan Pike being murdered? I saw this morning's paper. Is there no end to our troubles?" Etienne said dramatically while pacing the aisle.

"Hold on, 'Tienne. Let's get these calls out of the way and then get to the hospital. Dan can come back to our place and Beverly probably won't even hurt so much now that Tami's safe."

The phone rang just then. It was the manager of Pike's rink. I answered it. "Is Mr. Lepardieux there?"

"Sure, hold on," I gave the phone to him and left the office to go make the calls from the pros' room.

Ted, the tow truck driver came into the rink. "Hey, what am I supposed to do with that van? I don't guess I should take it away, should I?"

David guessed that no, he should leave it in the parking lot. Jonathan Martin drove in just at that moment to make sure the van was being left there. "Maybe now all these weird things will stop happening. It's been like a plague of locusts this past week. I think I could drive from here to Redwood City blindfolded, I've been back and forth so often."

He was walking around the van, noting the lack of license plates and its general shabbiness. "This thing shouldn't be allowed on the road. Even if it had plates. It's a death trap on its' way to happen!"

The lab team showed up finally and started going over the much-abused vehicle. The gritty, grey-black fingerprint powder was flying all over.

Harold Barker walked over to the deputy. "Is it all right if we leave? Do you need us?"

"Let's get all your names, phone numbers and addresses and then I guess you can go. Did you all see this van when you got here this morning?"

Everyone chorused, "Yes, we did."

"Okay. Give your names to Keith and then it's all right to go home. Not you, Berrien. I'll talk to you in a minute."

"Jonathan, I need to go inside for a couple of minutes." I did, too. The sweat from the dance session had soaked the skimpy skating dress, the orange juice had provided other problems. Given permission, I galloped down the hall to the pros room and its facilities.

A few minutes later, after a quick, warm shower and shedding the dress, putting only the jogging suit on, I re-emerged from the rink, clean and ready. "By the way, I'm supposed to pick Dan up at the hospital soon. Can we make this quick?"

"Don't worry, Berrien. He won't want to leave until he's sure that Tami's all right. He'll wait for you."

They were finished, for the time being, with the van and told the tow truck driver to go ahead and haul it to the police impound yard. It would be even more thoroughly checked there.

"Now, Berrien. We can start."

"Hey, I've just spent two hours skating. Let's at least go inside and sit down. Etienne must have some coffee going by now."

Settled comfortably in the pros' room, we started.

"You did see the van here when you came in the parking lot, didn't you?"

"Yes. I got here about eight thirty. There were a couple of other cars who turned in when I did. They had been right behind me since I left our house."

"Why didn't you call as soon as you got in the building?"

"It slipped my mind until Harold came in asking about it. Then I called. It didn't seem anything to be in a hurry about so I only called the office, not 911."

"You didn't hear any sound coming from it?"

"No. People frequently abandon junkers along the Coast. This was the first time we'd had one in our parking lot but it wasn't blocking traffic or anything."

"How did Ted hear her?"

"I don't know. I called to have it picked up and when we all came out of the rink, he was just getting ready to put the van on their truck. He said he thought he heard a voice. That's when he got the crowbar to open the back doors. And there Tami was! We were thrilled to see her—all dirty and messy but alive. It was wonderful!"

"Yeah. I bet it was. Okay. I'll let you get over to Carmichael. Will you take Tami to your place, too? Or back to her place?"

"Oh, I think we'd better take her to my place until everything is sorted out. I'll stop by her room and get some fresh clothes on my way. If you see Paul, tell him where she'll be, will you, please?"

"Sure."

"Thanks. I'll get going now, if it's okay with you."

The *N'ice Skates* Cherokee skidded into the parking lot just as I got to my car. Miki, Sheli and Mrs. Andrade tumbled out. "Where is she?" "Is she all right?" "Where has she been?"

I held up a hand. "Hold on. Stop. Take it easy. She appeared to be fine. She said she was fine, except hungry. She didn't know for sure where she had been. And last, but not least, we sent her to the hospital for a check-up and to see her parents. I'm on my way up to get her and Dan. Beverly will have to stay in the hospital another couple of days. She'll stay with me for a few days with her dad."

"She doesn't know who had her?" asked Sheli.

"No. I guess we'll have the FBI around all day asking her questions. If you want to do something useful, go to her place and get her some fresh clothes and bring them to my place later today. She couldn't wear any of mine. She's way too tall."

"Okay. We'll go get the clothes right now and see you soon." The three piled back into the car and squealed their way back onto the road, speeding, oblivious to the police contingent watching them. I could almost see them making mental notes about keeping a look-out for that Jeep from now on.

The trip to the hospital took a long time. Sunday visitors to the Coast were out in force. They would be. It was a fine, sunny Spring day, great scenery, good food, just right as a cure for the not-yet-summer blues. Californians are particularly prone to this malady. We expect sunshine and forget every winter that Madison Avenue's ideas on California are not the reality. As a result we generally sulk our way from the New Year's Day hangover until the sun has returned to us and we can go out and court skin cancer once more, usually around early April.

I parked my car in a back lot at the hospital, hoping that I could sneak in and find the Tompsons without a run-in with any journalists. To be sure, Etienne was going to have to give a full-fledged press conference and allow Tami and Paul some air time once the confusion was behind us and the crimes solved. I was tired of questions even as I was grateful that Tami was safe.

The door to the staff lounge opened just as I got there. Dipping my head, I scuttled in, hoping the resident thought I belonged there. He was probably tired after a twenty-four hour shift and after a short "Hi" he headed for his car, home and bed. Swearing at myself for wearing a hot pink jogging suit, a very visible target, I hurried inside, found a stairwell and climbed to the second floor.

Sounds of great hilarity were coming from a room four doors down the hall as I opened the corridor door. Paul heard the noise as the door slammed shut and poked his head out. "Hi, Berrien. Tami's here!"

"I know. Isn't it wonderful? Oh, Beverly, how's your leg feeling—never mind—stupid question. Miki and Sheli are on their way over to my place with some clothes, Tami. We think it would be a good idea for you to stay with me for a few days. Your dad is staying there, and so's Beverly as soon as we get her out of here."

Outside, in the main parking lot we could see a forest of antennas. Cameramen, announcers and print journalists were milling around, scrutinizing every car that drove in. As elusive as parking space for visitors usually is in hospital lots, I was certain that there were a lot of frustrated people driving around that piece of macadam.

A sheriff's car swung off the highway and drove around to the employees parking lot. Behind it, looking like a sedate, one owner, slightly older model car on Singin' Sam's used car lot, came a featureless medium blue-grey four door sedan. Both cars parked and the men and woman climbed out, Sean Mather from the county vehicle and the three FBI agents from the other one.

I looked around the crowded room. Dan was dressed in the clothes he had worn the day before. Some kind soul had washed the blood-stained shirt and he looked fairly presentable. Tami, face cleaned of sticky tape residue, hair still a mess and was still in clothes she had lived in for a week, Beverly still in her hospital-supplied nightwear, cast waving in the air.

Paul, dark circles under his eyes but otherwise presentable. The room was over-crowded now, to say nothing of having three large men and one formidable woman on their way up to it.

"Dan, are you discharged?"

"Yes, since earlier this morning. Just before you called about Tami."

"Why don't we meet the law out in the corridor and go back to my place? Tami can get a bath and change into fresh clothes and we can all be comfortable while she answers all their questions."

"Sounds good. Beverly, will you be all right? We'll come back later this evening."

"Of course, darling. I need some sleep, now, anyhow."

We heard voices in the hall. A lot of voices. Annoyed voices. The walls rattled as equipment banged into first one side and then the other of the walls. Nurses were shouting, "You can't come in here with that stuff. Get out of here."

Mr. Stanley finally stopped in his march to Beverly's room. About a dozen people plowed into him. I expected to see a "wave" or at least the first half of one as I poked my head out the door. Everyone managed to remain upright, though.

Stanley turned to face his retinue. "All of you, downstairs. There are sick people here. We will have a press conference when all of this is straightened out. Now, leave the hospital personnel in peace."

Grumbling, the press contingent turned around and tromped back to the elevators. I was surprised but pleasantly so. Dan and Tami stepped out into the hall to greet everyone. Then I went out and got Sean aside. "Don't you think it will be better if we all go to my house? All of this commotion is upsetting everyone in the hospital. We will even set up the press conference after you all talk to Tami. She'd like to get a bath and into some clean clothes."

"Let me check with the powers that be," Sean said. He had a short conference and then, "That would be great. Ms. Mosovich will go down and tell the media what's happening. We'll set the conference for five, if that's all right with you."

"Fine. My car's out where yours are. Let's go. Paul, how did you get here?"

"Drove. But I won't be able to get out until all those TV trucks are out of the way."

"Why don't you come with me? We can bring you back tonight when we come to see Beverly."

Everything arranged to almost everyone's satisfaction, the caravan began its trek back to my house. Misty, no doubt, would be pleased with the company, accepting it as my apology for leaving her alone for so long.

Paul, sitting in Misty's place, kept turning toward the back seat, checking constantly, still not quite believing that Tami was back, and safe. Dan had his arm around his daughter, his hand clutching her shoulder, then letting go and reclutching, trying to make certain that he wasn't dreaming.

Part of the nightmare was over. The kidnapper hadn't been caught but at least her parents, her partner and her friends had her back.

We all filed into the house. Sean had left a patrol car at the entrance to the driveway to keep the press at a distance until time for the announced meeting. The day was still beautiful and I led the band onto the deck. Sean and Paul got the plastic stacking chairs from the garage and we all sat down. I offered refreshments, coffee, tea, soft drinks. Everyone accepted except for Tami who disappeared into the bathroom for a shower just as Miki, Sheli and Mrs. Andrade arrived bringing some fresh clothes for her.

While everyone waited for Tami, Sean filled the federal agents in on last night's happenings at the hospital and I explained what had happened earlier in the day at the arena.

As soon as Tami had sat down, hair still wet, struggling to regain its natural curl, the questions came fast and furious from the FBI agents.

"Did you recognize your kidnapper?"

"No, but there were almost always two people around. They wore masks when they came in the room where they kept me. But it was Vaughan Pike who came to my place. He said he needed to talk to me. I didn't want to be rude so I went with him. We got in his car and drove to one of the picnic areas. He had some coffee in a thermos. We sat in his car and drank some. There must have been some funny stuff in the coffee. That's all I remember 'til I woke up in a strange room."

"Then what? Did you hear any voices you could recognize?"

"Mr. Pike wasn't there, if that's what you mean. I saw him attacking you, Berrien when they showed it on television. There was a set in the room. It was a small bedroom. One voice sounded sort of familiar but I've got no idea who it was. There were two men. But when I did the tapes, they would come in the room with real bright lights, shining in my eyes, so I couldn't see behind the lights. One was real tall, I think and the other was shorter. The lights were at different heights."

"Were the two men always there?"

"No. I think some times one of them went out. There was a window in the room but it only opened onto some sort of brick wall across a narrow shaft of some sort. I couldn't see anything except the wall. Oh. There were four windows like mine below me. And when I had the window open, I could smell coffee being roasted."

"What could you hear outside?"

"Just faint traffic sounds. All muffled. I guess because of that shaft."

"Were there any windows above yours?"

"No. I think this place must have been on a top floor. There were never any people sounds above me."

"Let's go back to your coffee time with Pike. Did you see any other people or cars at the picnic area? And do you know which spot you stopped at?"

"There was a fancy Porsche parked near us. Nobody was in it, though. At least not that I could see. There was a man walking down on the beach, though. He looked very tall and skinny but he was all bundled up. He sure didn't look like he'd be driving a Porsche, though. You know. I always think of sports car drivers as windswept, no hat, casual clothes, that sort of thing."

"Did you see the license plate of that car?"

"I saw it. I don't know the numbers but it was green and white, looked like snow covered mountains." She thought for a minute. "Oh, I bet they were Colorado plates!"

"Very likely. Now, did these two men try to harm you in anyway?"

"You mean, like rape me? No. They brought food every day. Not very healthy stuff, though. Doughnuts for breakfast with orange juice and coffee. All from some coffee shop. The name was always on the bags. The Sugar Shell! That's it. That's what it was called."

"Excuse me, Ms. Gamble, may I use your phone?" asked Ms. Mosovich.

"Of course." I handed her the portable I had brought out on the deck.

"No. I'll go inside and use one of the others," she said as she got up.

"What about other meals? More fast food?" continued Mr. Stanley.

"Yes. In fact I never even want to see a Happy Hamburger burger again! Their milk shakes are good, though."

"Did you hear any of the conversations these men had?"

"No. Not really. They didn't talk loudly, or argue. At least not that I heard. They may have put something in the soft drink at night because I'd eat and just fall asleep. I never even made it through the six o'clock news."

"What about yesterday? Did you get the regular meals?"

"Well, breakfast, yes. But I didn't have my watch on. Mr. Pike had come by my place early Monday. I had just gotten up and was thinking about going running so I hadn't put it on yet. Then, I'm sure lunch was very late and it was a deli sandwich instead of a hamburger. I don't remember getting any dinner."

"Were the men still in the apartment all day? Did you hear them go out at all?"

"At least one went out, maybe both of them. It was after I had the sandwich. I remember that. Then, much later, it was after Wide World of Sports was over, they came back in—or one of them did. They brought me a bottle of wine, not full, already opened. But they would, wouldn't they? Open it, I mean. After all, I didn't have a corkscrew. I drank a glass of it."

"Then what?"

"I don't remember anything until I was rattling around in that van. It seemed like I was in that thing for hours. I think we even drove over some dirt roads, rutted, you know. I had a horrible headache. Finally, we came to a stop. We were parked on level ground and I could hear the ocean. Then, another car pulled up. I could hear the tires squeal. Like the driver was making a tight turn, or something. Then the van shook as a door slammed. I heard another door close and then a loud engine roaring, going away."

"What happened then?"

"Well, I tried to thump—on the van wall—with my feet. It hurt my head. I found some rough pieces of carpet so I rolled around and scratched on it to try and get the tape off my mouth. Boy, does that stuff stick! I heard more cars come and park close by but I guess between the traffic on the road and the ocean, no one heard me pounding on the walls. I knew I had to get that stuff off my mouth so I just kept working at it."

Tami stopped talking for a minute to take a big gulp of her iced tea. Dan reached over and patted her shoulder, more to reassure himself, I think, than Tami.

"Then all of a sudden," she continued, "I felt the van being moved, sort of like being lifted. I was afraid someone was trying to roll it into the ocean. That's when I called out. Actually, I was trying to scream but it didn't come out very loud. The rest you know."

We all fell silent for a minute. Suddenly, I remembered the Porsche that had gone past me into Half Moon Bay in the morning. It had been the only car going in that direction. I was sure there had been two men in it and told the agents about it.

"Can you identify them, Ms. Gamble?" asked Mr. Watson, who had been silent up until now.

"No. I didn't pay attention to it."

"Okay, Tami," said Mr. Stanley. "Let's go back—no, just in your mind," he hurriedly added as he saw her start in fear. "Just give us all you can remember of sounds outside the place where you were held."

"Oh, I couldn't hear much. I watched TV most of the time. I guess just a fog horn, mostly when I woke up in the morning. Oh, and a ding-ding sound. Was that maybe a cable car?"

"Could be," he said. "That's what we think it is."

Ms. Mosovich came back from her stint on the telephone. "The Sugar Shell exists. It's down near the Bay. And there's only one. It's not a chain. About a block from Powell Street. You could hear the cable cars and the fog horns around there. There's a lot of apartment houses there, though. One of the agents has gone down there with the descriptions Berrien gave last night. The two guys who were in Pike's room. They must be the same two. He'll call us back."

The telephone startled us and it slid off my lap with a loud clatter onto the deck. I picked it up quickly. "Is Sean Mather there?" asked a gruff, unfamiliar voice. I handed Sean the phone.

"Sean Mather here." He listened, head cocked to one side. If he hadn't been such a big man he would have looked like a bird, listening for a worm. "You're kidding! God! Am I stupid! We should have guessed right away. Okay. Thanks."

Sean looked at all of us then said in a disgusted voice, "You know those prints, the ex-con Richard Wellington? The ones we found all over the rink?"

"Yes. What about them?"

"Richard Wellington is Trick Brewster! Those prints of his I took yesterday match Wellington's."

"Of course, that's whose voice it was!" Tami and I said almost in unison.

The FBI agents asked me where he lived. I didn't know exactly and said so. "I know he lives in the City. He said so the other day. Call the rink. Etienne has his personnel file. He'll have the address."

"Let's go inside and use the land line phone. Do you, by any chance have two lines here?" asked Mr. Watson.

"Three, actually. One's an Internet line but there's a regular phone hooked up to it."

The lawmen—and woman—stampeded into the house, picking up phones as they reached one.

Sean dialled the rink. Etienne answered it himself. Poor man. None of us had called him to give him a report on Tami. "Etienne, get me Trick Brewster's home address. Right now, please."

"Powell Street?" Sean confirmed. "Okay." He wrote it down and hurried to Mr. Watson. "Here's his home address. Now what? We have to call the San Francisco police, don't we?"

"Yes. I'll do that now. They can send a couple of officers right now to watch the place. We'll get going. You're coming, aren't you?"

"You bet I am. Just let me call in to the office and give them the new information."

"Hey!" I shouted, trying to be heard in the confusion. "What about the news conference you all promised the media. They're still lined up out there, waiting."

"Oh, don't worry about them. They'll follow us as soon as we leave. Just watch 'em," promised Mr. Watson. "Maybe we'll get lucky and they'll run out of gas."

Sean got in his cruiser and the FBI agents piled into their car and peeled out of the driveway after Sean stopped to tell the young man at the gate to stay there and not let anyone in.

"Tami, maybe you'd like to call your mother and tell her the latest. She had said that Trick looked a little bit familiar to her. It will probably make her feel better to know what we know."

"Yes, I bet it will. I'll go call now."

"Dan, why don't you go take a nap? You look exhausted. There's nothing we can do but wait."

"That's a good idea."

I glanced out front. Mr. Watson was right. Not a television truck was in sight. Not even our local reporter was left out by the highway. It was quiet. The telephone wasn't even ringing.

Mrs. Andrade sat down on the couch next to me. "Do you think that man killed Tomaso? He wasn't a good brother for many years, but he was my brother."

"I'm pretty sure of it. Otherwise, it would be too coincidental. He probably wanted to see Miki or Sheli and was in the wrong place at the wrong time."

"Come on, Mom. We ought to go home. We have the funeral tomorrow. You look like you could use some rest, yourself," Sheli commented.

The Andrade family left and I just sat, Misty back in her accustomed spot on the couch with her head and shoulders on my lap. I dozed along with her.

Chapter 19

The phone woke me. I struggled to get up, stiff from sleeping sitting up with my neck all kinked up. "Hello."

"Berrien, it's Sean Mather. May I come over and see you and the two Tompsons?"

"Sure. What happened? Did you catch Trick and Vernon?"

Tami and Dan came into the room, rubbing sleep from their eyes and looked at me with question marks in their eyes.

"It's Sean. He's coming here," I said to them. Then back to Sean, "When will you be here? Where are you now?"

"I'm at the main police station in San Francisco. It'll take me about an hour to get finished here, then thirty minutes to drive down. I'll explain everything when I get there."

"Great. We'll see you then."

It occurred to me that we hadn't had either lunch or dinner. I got up and started rummaging through the refrigerator. "How would you two like a Denver omelet? That's about all we have that I can fix fast."

Dan agreed to it and so did Tami. Soon we were tripping over each other, setting the table and cooking. Misty got in the act, too, reminding me that she hadn't been fed either.

We were all silent as we ate. I turned on the local television news. There was nothing on about any kind of police action in San Francisco. No traffic tie-ups, which are the inevitable result of any problems in the City, even on a week-end. Only a shooting in Marin County, and a big rig overturned on a freeway, spilling toxic material all over. Pictures of men running around the mess dressed in HAZMAT suits with a final identification of the material. It was a truckload of soap powder.

After what seemed a year, we heard a car pull into the driveway. Sean looked beat as he came in and sat down. I offered him a drink but he shook his head. "If I had one now, you'd have another house guest for the night. But thanks."

"Well, what happened? Did you catch Trick or Richard or whoever he is? Has he confessed to anything?"

In answer, he handed all three of us copies of a handwritten letter and sank back, exhausted onto the couch.

To Whoever Finds Us
We have decided that this is the only way out for us. We have no hope for the future. Both of us learned just yesterday that we are HIV positive. It was a great shock. Since we would, no doubt, be arrested for several actions of ours in the past week, our suicides will save everyone a great deal of trouble.
I am Richard Wellington, not Trick Brewster. I am an ex-convict. After I got out of prison I met a man who offered me a job at his home as a caretaker. It was Vaughan Pike. We became lovers. He swore to me that he was not ill. He didn't know that

I had been in prison for a year or so. Then, I let something slip about my past and he threw me out of his house.
I came to San Francisco and started a new life, with new, faked identification as Trick Brewster. I worked as a weight trainer in several gyms. Then I heard about the job at the new ice arena on the Coast. It sounded like a great place, with a chance for me to get a free cottage once things got going. I applied, using fake credentials that I made up after several visits to well-known physical therapy clinics in the area. I got hired. Everyone there treated me good and I promised myself I'd go straight and do a really good job.
There was a group picture taken not long after the rink opened. It was published in a magazine called Skating. Pike saw it, of course, and recognized me. At least that's what he told me just a few weeks ago.
He called me last month and said I owed him for not reporting me to the people at the rink. He wanted me to kidnap the new pairs team that the Andrade twins had. He said they were his team. I told him no. Then he said he would tell Etienne who I was and what I was if I didn't do what he told me to.
Vernon and I talked it over. We didn't see that we had any choice. So when he called back, I said I'd do it if he promised me that there wouldn't be any rough stuff. He agreed.
The plan was for me to get them Sunday night as they left the arena after their private ice time. I had keys to the rink but I knew the Zamboni door was always open when there were skaters in the rink. I decided to go in that way. Then Miki and Sheli wouldn't see me. I'm sorry about the old man. He saw me and tried to get me to give him some money. He'd been drinking from a wine bottle he had in his hands. I told him I didn't have any money, to go away. He wouldn't go so I grabbed him to turn him around and give him a shove. His

scarf got caught and tangled up in my watch strap. He struggled to get free but just kept wrapping it tighter around my arm. I guess that's how he got strangled. At least, he fell down and I couldn't get him to get up, so I left him out by the trash bin.
By the time this was over, the twins and Tami and Paul had left. I threw the bottle in the trash and then dragged the old man around to the front, let myself in and then put him on the ice. I figured it would give me time to set up an alibi. That the time of death wouldn't be identifiable.
The next morning, Pike, Vernon and I had a talk. We decided for Pike to go get Tami and we'd just keep her a couple of days. Pike thought up the whole scheme. It didn't make much sense to me and Vernon but we went along with it. When he had his heart attack Wednesday night we didn't know what to do. We made the second tape, hoping that we could talk to him that day.
Then I heard Etienne talking on the phone with Pike's doctor. I heard about the AIDS medicine. I came home and told Vernon. We got tested right away. That new two day special test. Both of us were positive. We went to see Pike at the hospital. I lost my temper, I was so scared, for me and for Vernon. I started pounding on his chest. I didn't mean to kill him but I guess I did. I'm not sorry about him.

(signed) Richard Brewster Wellington
We were all silent after we read this. What a pitiful missive.
"Does Etienne know yet?" I asked Sean.
"No, I have to see him now. The whole story will be in the paper tomorrow, though. There wasn't anything we could do to stop it. We all gathered out in the street before going up to their apartment with the

television people there and everything. The two guys were lying in the kitchen. The stove was on. We could smell the gas as soon as we got up the stairs. The three other tenants on the floor were unconscious, too. If we hadn't gotten there when we did, those people would have died, too. And the building blown up or on fire, most likely. Screwups, that's what they were, from start to finish."

"How awful. But how lucky those other people were. You can be thankful that you helped some people."

"Yeah, I guess. Well, I've got to go see Etienne, and then Mrs. Andrade." Sean left and got wearily in his car to finish what had started one week before with such useless violence.

Chapter 20

I paced the sound room restlessly, Misty Joy keeping pace with me. The last night of the show was about to begin. It had better be good. Philip and Trent were here. Trent was complete with his video camera to record the show for posterity, or my grandkids, whichever came first.

The two dress rehearsals had been disasters. I know that there is a quaint saying in show business about bad dress rehearsals meaning a good show. I never counted on it. They had been scheduled as complete run-throughs. Ha! It took four hours to do the first half. My temper more than matched Etienne's legendary flare-ups at other shows. I know. I had seen his tantrums but not for all the tea at Tetley's could I contain myself. The second one ran just under five hours. It took longer because I had to set the Grande Finale.

We had opened on Thursday night to a full house. In fact, all of the performances had been sold out early. I guess all the unfortunate publicity we had gotten a couple of months earlier had been useful after all. We had toyed with adding a couple more shows but too many skaters had already scheduled their vacations right after the Sunday night performance. It was, after all, the third week-end in June.

Thursday night we had managed the two hour and fifteen minute show in three and a half hours, cutting a considerable amount of time off the dress rehearsals but still too long. Friday night we did better, just under three hours. Ariadne had performed miracles with the backstage crews. Mrs. Simeon, in her persona as wardrobe mistress, was wonderful, staying after the shows to check all the costumes, sew on missing buttons, sequins, beads and lace, spot clean any chewing gum or lipstick and press the costumes that had gotten wrinkled when thrown on the floor during a quick change.

Saturday afternoon went well, too. Saturday night was another story. Under Murphy's Law, if anything can go wrong, it will. It did. We started out the evening with a power failure for the whole Coast which lasted for thirty minutes. And that was the good part. A pair of girls were skating their number to *San Antonio Stroll* with life-size dummies attached to their skates and hands. About half way through the number, "George" lost his stuffing—white cotton all over the white ice. We had to stop the show and clean the ice.

Dorothy, who so far had managed to miss Toto, decapitated him in the "Road to Oz" number, fell and said some very improper things in a voice loud enough to have been heard in San Francisco. In the same number, the bubble machine went haywire and spilled the soap suds all over the little tots.

And that was just the first half!

I put on the headset that connected me to all the crew. Spots ready. House lights ready. Music ready. Backstage ready. I called, "Blackout." Then, "Start the music."

The sounds of the overture to the first half sailed out over the audience. The skaters in the "Vision of the Orient" number skated onto the ice to take up their starting positions.

Taking a deep breath I called for, "Lights. Spots on white gel." The show had started. The production number went well, in fact perfectly. No one missed a cue, all the solos were well-applauded and Brandi was in the costume I had picked out. I had heard rumors that her mother was going to get her into the beaded chandelier number and had left instructions with both Mrs. Simeon and Ariadne to make sure she had the right costume on.

The first half finished on time and I heaved a sigh of relief. Even the bubble machine had minded its manners and there was an adorable scene when one of the little boys forgot to go with his group because he was following one of the bubbles. In fact he followed it clear off the ice and into the audience.

"House lights."

Everyone got up and stretched, wandered around. I was still antsy. Marguerita's number was in the second half and her mother was here to watch her daughter skate for the first time, ever. She had been doing beautifully. I just hoped she didn't get nervous because of her mom.

"Five minutes," my announcer called.

"Two minutes." Everyone hurried to get to their seats for the second half.

I waited for the stragglers to get settled. We didn't want any accidents in the audience. Climbing on open bleachers is tricky at best and some of the customers were no longer in the first bloom of youth.

"Blackout," I ordered as the second half overture began. The ballet number, "A Night in Old Vienna" was next. I knew Ariadne would be peeking through the curtains. So far the girls had managed to go to the right (or left) direction every time and mostly in time to the music. A minor miracle. "Spots on. Green gel, numbers one and three. White gel, numbers two and four." The waltz number ran right behind the girls, with beautiful steps devised by David, ladies in long waltz gowns, opera length gloves and the men in white tie and tails. And we were on our way to the Grande Finale.

Marguerita performed like a seasoned veteran, hands clapping, head moving in time to the music while her feel flew in the routine we had set. Next came Snow White skating to *Some Day My Prince Will Come*.

"Spots, stay away from the curtain." I knew I had requested the same thing five times before but it was necessary. Teresa moved fluidly to the lovely music. Her costume was just like the cartoon's Snow White dress. As the music came to the end, she did a long spiral down the ice toward the curtain. "Spots, stay on her." Then she stood up and hugged her prince, a Teresa-sized *Kermit the Frog* wearing a golden crown. As I had predicted, it was a hit.

The Senior Octet looked gorgeous in the costumes Mrs. Simeon and the ladies had made up. They were truly much better than the ones we had originally ordered. The Russian number worked just right tonight, too. The intricate movements developed by David were impressive, without confusing the inexperienced skaters. We had dispensed with the props meant to look like Russian church steeples. They had, under the black light we were using for most of the number, looked more like phallic symbols!

The final group number was the Senior Drill Team. A smart, high-stepping and fast group of young ladies looked excited to be out there. As the show came to its conclusion, the special number was Tami and Paul, the United States Pair Champions, skating their new exhibition number. The lift that Miki and Sheli had invented for them drew gasps of awe and several screams of fear, one of them mine, I am ashamed to admit.

The curtain was moving as if in a windstorm. The whole cast, all two hundred and five of them were gathering back stage for the Grande Finale. As the music began, they came out in order of appearance as much as could be arranged. The entire surface of the ice was covered with a kaleidoscope of color. "Spots, pan over the ice, over them all."

Suddenly, my music man took my headset off and Tami and Paul burst into the room and carried me onto the ice, leaving the door open.

The dancers came forward and presented me with a bouquet of roses. Teresa whispered shyly to me, "There are two hundred and five there."

The soloists lined up, with me in high heels in the center, to do a "wave bow," just like my dream. We did it very well, except for my whimpers of pain as the sharply barbed roses poked into my ribcage.

The entire cast began to bow gracefully as we had taught them. A white blur of fur streaked out onto the ice and gleefully greeted all of her friends as she slid among the massed cast. The whole group was quickly turned into two hundred and six bowling pins with Misty as the ball as we all went down in a heap with perfect wave timing.

BLACK OUT

About the Author

Joan Bartlett has been an ice skater (still is as Berrien could tell you), an ice skating judge and a professional ice skating coach. She has produced, directed and choreographed numerous amateur ice skating shows, one of which is the background for "N'ice Shows." She lives with her husband and her proto-type Akitador in Foster City, California.

Printed in the United States
29388LVS00004B/345